Bhangra Babes

Other novels by Narinder Dhami
you will enjoy:

Bindi Babes
Bollywood Babes

Bhangra Babes

◊ narinder dhami ◊

DELACORTE PRESS

Published by
Delacorte Press
an imprint of
Random House Children's Books
a division of Random House, Inc.
New York

Visit us on the Web! www.randomhouse.com/kids
Educators and librarians, for a variety of teaching tools,
visit us at www.randomhouse.com/teachers

Library of Congress Cataloging-in-Publication Data

Dhami, Narinder.
Bhangra babes / Narinder Dhami.
p. cm.
Summary: As their auntie's wedding day approaches, the Indian-British Dhillon sisters try to
rescue her from her fiancé's meddling aunt while also competing against one another for the
affections of the new, handsome boy at school.
ISBN 0-385-73318-6 (trade) — ISBN 0-385-90337-5 (lib. bdg.)
[1. Sisters—Fiction. 2. Aunts—Fiction. 3. Weddings—Fiction. 4. East Indians—Great Britain—
Fiction. 5. Schools—Fiction. 6. England—Fiction. 7. Humorous stories.] I. Title.
PZ7.D54135Bha 2005
[Fic]—dc22   2005041333

The text of this book is set in 12-point Palatino.

Printed in the United States of America

April 2006

10 9 8 7 6 5 4 3 2 1

BVG

For Robert

chapter 1

"**D**o you think it will hurt?" Jazz asked.
"No, of course not," I said briskly. "Now
stick your leg out."

"It's got to hurt a bit," Geena remarked. She was
painting her nails at the dressing table. "Pulling hairs
out by the roots usually does."

"The box says it's quick and easy and painless," I
replied, picking up a waxed strip.

"They're hardly going to say it's quick and easy and
hurts like hell, are they?" Geena pointed out.

"That's true." Now Jazz was looking worried.

"Oh, live a bit dangerously for once," I said,
advancing on Jazz with the wax strip held out in front
of me. But Jazz rolled over to the other side of the bed
and tucked her bare legs underneath her.

"Why do I have to be the one to try it first?" she grumbled.

"Because Geena and I value your opinion," I said. This might have worked if Geena hadn't giggled. "You don't want to turn up for the first day of the new term tomorrow with hairy legs, do you?"

"No one's going to be looking at my legs," Jazz said with satisfaction, glancing at herself in the mirror. She'd gone up a whole cup size over the summer holidays. Now she was bigger than I was. Drat and double drat. How embarrassing is it when your little sister looks older than you do?

"Anyway"—Jazz was eager to change the subject—"I thought one of us was going to sneak downstairs to listen at the living room door."

Geena tutted loudly.

"I don't know what you're being so uppity about," I said. "It was your idea."

"She thinks she's one of the chosen few now she's moving to the upper school," Jazz sniffed. "Saint Geena the Perfect."

"It's because I'm growing up," Geena said, waving her hands in the air to dry her pale pink polish. "I simply can't afford to behave so childishly anymore."

"So if I thump you, you won't retaliate?" I asked, grabbing Jazz's pillow and swinging it round my head like a hammer thrower.

"I will, of course, defend myself with whatever comes to hand," Geena replied, picking up a hairbrush.

"Oh, stop it, you two," Jazz said in a world-weary

voice. "Let's talk about Auntie. What are we going to do with her?"

This was a question we'd been asking ourselves ever since Auntie had moved in with us. Our mum had died a year and a half ago, and Auntie had come from India to look after us and Dad. It all looks so simple, written down in one sentence like that. It doesn't tell you anything about the pain and the suffering. And I'm not just talking about Mum, which was the worst thing ever. We also had to learn how to get along with Auntie taking her place. There's only one thing you need to know about Auntie. She interferes. That is all.

"I *mean*"—Jazz was getting warmed up—"we hand her the best-looking teacher in our school on a plate—"

"I'd say Mr. Arora is possibly the best-looking teacher in the whole of London," I broke in.

"Or even the entire country," Geena suggested.

"All right," Jazz went on. "We hand her possibly the best-looking teacher in the whole country on a plate—"

"We didn't exactly hand him to her on a plate," Geena interrupted.

"Oh-ho, did we not?" I scoffed. "Whose idea was it to get them together in the first place?"

"Yours." Geena gave me a look. "And as I remember, they had a quarrel the very first time they met."

"Details," I said airily. "They soon realized they were meant for each other."

"Was that before or after the Molly Mahal disaster?" asked Geena.

Three or four months ago there was a bit of a rift

between Auntie and Mr. Arora when we had ex-Bollywood star Molly Mahal staying with us for a while. Don't ask why and how—it's too complicated to explain. And definitely don't ask Geena and Jazz, because they'll blame me. I mean. As if.

"All right," Jazz said impatiently. "We find possibly the best-looking teacher in the country and we try our hardest to get him and Auntie together—"

"We did more than try," I said. "We actually did it."

Auntie and Mr. Arora had been stepping out together since the Bollywood party at school, just after Molly Mahal had callously abandoned us to resume her *filmi* career. Now what we all wanted to know was, when was the wedding? Which was why we wanted to find out what was going on at this very minute behind our living room door.

"Please stop interrupting me," Jazz said huffily. "I mean, we've done all that and made it really easy for them. So *when* are they going to get married?"

"Jazz, you've been asking the same thing for the last three months," Geena grumbled.

"Well, when *are* they?" Jazz persisted. "I mean, Mr. Arora's got that promotion now—"

"He'll be fantastic as head of the lower school," I said. "Much better than Mr. Grimwade was. Although now he's the deputy head, Mr. Grimwade has the potential to create a lot more misery."

"So what's stopping Auntie and Mr. Arora from announcing their engagement?" Jazz persisted.

"That's not for us to say," Geena replied, quite

pompously actually. "And there's nothing we can do about it either, except wait and see."

"Oh, I wouldn't say that," I remarked.

"Really?" Geena said frostily. "And why wouldn't you say that, Amber?"

"Oh, God." Jazz put her hands to her temples. "I can sense one of Amber's ridiculous ideas coming. I feel sick."

"I'm not going to *do* anything," I said cheerfully. "Except maybe drop a few subtle hints."

I lifted my pillow and picked up the magazine that was hidden underneath it.

"*Asian Bride*," said Geena. "Yes, very subtle. Like being hit on the head with a hammer."

"I thought I'd just leave it lying around," I explained. "No pressure. Now"—I picked up the waxed strip again—"let's get on with this, shall we?"

"I'm not going first," Jazz stated firmly.

I sighed. "Well, *really*. I sometimes wonder if I'm the only one with any sense of adventure round here."

"The three of us do it together or not at all," said Jazz.

"Oh, if you say so." I peeled off one of the strips and slapped it onto Jazz's leg. Then I stuck one to my own.

"Not me," Geena said. "My nails are still wet."

"Too late," I replied, bouncing across the bed to stick a strip on Geena's shin.

"It's not hurting at the moment," Jazz remarked cautiously.

"Of course not," I said. "I told you it wouldn't. Now, one, two, three—pull."

5

I think Jazz must have torn hers off a fraction of a second before I did because a bloodcurdling scream echoed around the room.

"*Aaaaaaaarrgh!*"

No, not that one. That was me.

Oh, every-rude-word-you-can-think-of-and-then-some.

The pain. *The pain*. It was like a million tiny red-hot needles piercing the skin. I was lucky I had any skin left, mind you.

"You said it wouldn't hurt!" Jazz wailed, rubbing the red patches on her legs.

Still shaking, I realized that there'd only been two screams. Not three. I looked down. Geena's strip was still stuck to her leg.

"Get that off right now," I ordered.

"I can't," Geena spluttered, looking utterly terrified. "My nails are still wet."

"Allow me," I said with grim relish, and whipped the strip off at speed. Geena's screech nearly brought the roof down on us.

We heard footsteps charging up the stairs, and Auntie flung the door open.

"What is it?" she gasped. "Who's been hurt?"

"Amber tried to kill me!" Jazz moaned.

"I nearly killed myself too," I said defensively.

Auntie surveyed the scene in front of her, our bare legs with the red patches and the wax strips covered with hairs. She smirked. "Don't be such big babies," she said. "Leg waxing doesn't hurt. Try a bikini wax. Now *that's* painful."

"Can we not go there?" Geena said faintly. "I've just had the most horrible picture come into my head."

"I've still got hairy bits," Jazz grumbled, inspecting her legs closely.

"You can tweezer those out," Auntie replied.

"*Tweezer* them out?" Jazz shrieked. "Are you insane?"

"I was impressed when you said you were coming up here to get ready for school tomorrow." With one sweeping glance, Auntie took in the makeup, the hair dryers, the straightening irons, the nail varnish and all the other stuff strewn on the bed. "I kind of had the idea that you were going to lay your uniforms out and pack your school bags and check over your summer assignments. Little things like that."

Looking justifiably smug, I pulled my bag out from under the bed and held it up. "I checked my holiday homework yesterday, my bag's packed and my uniform is hanging up in the wardrobe," I said. "We're ready to go, aren't we, girls?"

"Oh, yes," said Geena in a fake cheerful voice.

"I've just got to sort out my uniform," Jazz muttered, carefully pushing her school skirt under the bed with her toe.

"I can never count on you two to back me up," I grumbled.

"Well done, Amber," Auntie said, smiling. "And you still have time to read magazines, I see."

Asian Bride lay on my pillow. I'd forgotten to hide it again after showing the others.

"Oh, yes, that," I blustered. "I—er—like the—um—pictures."

"Really." Auntie picked up the magazine and flipped through it while Jazz and Geena pulled gleeful faces and made throat-slashing gestures at me.

"If you don't mind, I'd like to borrow it." Auntie moved over to the door, taking the magazine with her. "I need to start making plans, now that Jai and I have agreed to get married."

"What?" we shrieked.

Looking pleased with herself, Auntie disappeared downstairs.

"Wait!" I yelled, trying to fight my way off the bed past Jazz. "Give us details!"

"Get your foot out of my ear, Amber!" Jazz shouted. "Did you hear that? They're getting married!"

"I don't believe it!" Geena wailed. "I've smudged my nails!"

I was first to the door, but Jazz was breathing down my neck. Geena followed us, grabbing a box of nail wipes. We clattered downstairs like a horde of rampaging wildebeest, intent on clearing everything out of our path. This was big. This was *huge*!

Mr. Arora was sitting in the living room next to Auntie, looking embarrassed but very happy. Dad was there too, a big grin on his face.

"Calm down, girls," Auntie said as the three of us hurtled into the room. "You're frightening your uncle-to-be."

We all beamed at Mr. Arora, who did actually look

a little scared. He was staring nervously at me, and it was only then that I remembered I'd borrowed Auntie's giant heated rollers and they were stuck all over my head—I looked like a porcupine.

"Isn't it great news, girls?" Dad said, his eyes shining. He took his glasses off and wiped them furiously. He's such an old softie, I think he might have been about to burst into tears. "Are you pleased?"

"I should say so," Jazz replied enthusiastically. "It's about time!"

Geena elbowed her in the ribs. "You old romantic, you."

"Well, it *is* about time," Jazz said defensively. "I mean, she's fancied him for ages, and—"

"Shall we end this conversation right here?" Auntie suggested.

Mr. Arora blushed. He was so good-looking (floppy-dark-hair-and-melting-chocolate-brown-eyes kind of good-looking), but he really didn't seem to know it. Bless him.

"Congratulations," I said. "Does this mean you won't give me any maths homework from now on?"

"Sadly, no," Mr. Arora replied.

"You'll be able to give us loads of insider information, though, won't you?" Geena said with glee. "You can be our spy in the school camp."

"When's the wedding?" asked Jazz. "Everyone at school will want to see the pictures." Her eyes shone with a mercenary gleam. "We could charge."

"There you are." Auntie smiled at her new fiancé.

"Didn't I tell you that there's no way the girls would try to exploit this situation?"

They stared into each other's eyes for a moment, and it was very sweet. Dad pretended to cough and I handed him a tissue.

"The wedding will be in six weeks' time," Auntie went on. "We have some arrangements to discuss with Jai's parents first, so we're keeping it a secret for the next few days." She gave us a stern look. "Don't tell anyone just yet."

"Discretion is our middle name," I said loftily.

"No, trouble is your middle name, Amber," replied Auntie. "But make sure that this time you do as you're told."

"We will," Geena promised. "I'll keep these two blabbermouths in line."

"And I hope you'll forgive me, girls," Mr. Arora added.

"What for?" Jazz asked.

"For taking your aunt away when you've just got to know her," he replied.

Dad hiccupped and reached for another tissue. I wasn't about to burst into tears, but I was shocked. *Of course* Auntie would be moving out after she married Mr. Arora. It was something I hadn't really thought much about before this.

But how did I feel about it?

How did any of us feel?

chapter 2

"**O**f course, we had much more fun before Auntie came," Jazz said dreamily. It was the next morning, and she was stuffing books into her schoolbag higgledy-piggledy. "Remember? We ate takeaways all the time and watched TV until midnight and Dad was never here, so we did whatever we liked."

"Yes, but were we happy?" Geena asked.

"Hold on a moment." I leaned across the kitchen table and flicked my fingers across the top of Geena's head. "Your halo's a little off-center."

"How childish," Geena said tartly. "That's exactly why I wouldn't expect you two to understand what I mean."

"I'm not childish," Jazz retorted, sticking her tongue out.

Geena looked smug. "I rest my case."

"I know what you're getting at," I said impatiently. "We were only doing all that stuff because of Mum, so we weren't really happy at all."

After Mum died, our family had almost fallen apart. Geena, Jazz and I had stuck together because that was what we always did, but we'd never talked about Mum. We'd tried to pretend it had never happened and that we were all right really. Dad had coped by staying at work all the time. How had we got ourselves out of that mess? We hadn't. Auntie had got us out of it.

"Things will be different this time, anyway," Geena said wisely. "Dad doesn't spend so much time at work, for one thing." She glanced at the clock. "We'd better go."

"If Auntie leaves, we'll have to do our own cooking and cleaning," Jazz grumbled.

"I'll miss you too." Auntie came into the kitchen in her dressing gown, a towel wrapped round her hair. "Have a nice day."

"You too," I replied, adding cheekily, "Are you seeing your fiancé later?"

"That's for me to know and you to find out," Auntie replied.

"How childish," Geena muttered.

"Oh, be quiet," I said. "I *am* a child. I'm allowed to be childish."

"I was talking to Auntie," said Geena.

"I think it's time you all left for school," Auntie said. "And remember"—she followed us down the hall toward the front door—"don't say a word to anyone. It's still a secret."

"Yes, but for how long?" I wondered, closing the door behind us. "You know what it's like round here. Word travels faster than the speed of light."

"Oh! There you are, girls."

Our elderly neighbor, Mrs. Macey, popped out of the house next door. I swear she'd been standing looking through the letter box, waiting for us to come out. Mrs. Macey is Auntie's biggest and most faithful fan, even though just a little while ago, she hated us all simply for being Indian.

"Isn't it wonderful?" she breathed reverently. "But I'm not going to say another word about it, girls. My lips are sealed!"

And she popped back inside again.

"Did she mean what I think she meant?" asked Jazz.

"Yes," Geena said.

"But how does she know?" Jazz persisted.

"Auntie must have told her," I replied, opening the gate.

"But *we're* not allowed to tell anyone?" Jazz grumbled. "That's so unfair."

At that moment we were distracted as a bicycle flew across the pavement and screeched to a halt inches from our toes. Without so much as an apology, a hulking great Neanderthal climbed off the bike and thrust Dad's *Daily Telegraph* under my nose.

Now, in the past I've had my problems with the kids who deliver our newspapers. I admit it. Leo, our last paperboy, and I had a love-hate kind of relationship going on. But Leo had gone to America with his family for six months. Now, apparently, we had some kind of skinhead person who was built like a tank delivering our newspapers.

I stepped away from the *Daily Telegraph*. "Excuse me," I said. "That's not my job."

"What?" The paper person stared at me blankly. I realized now that it was a girl, but her broad shoulders, short-cropped hair and combat trousers made it difficult to tell. "It's your paper, isn't it?"

"There's the front door." I pointed at the house. "You have to go and push it through the letter box. Those are the rules."

The girl glared at me. "It's your paper, and I'm giving it to *you*," she snapped.

A gold stud glinted at me from the middle of her tongue. I stared at it with interest. I'd never met an Indian girl (or boy) under the age of sixteen who was allowed to have a tongue stud. It was *so* not done.

"But I'm on my way out," I said politely. "All you've got to do is walk down the path and push it through our door."

"All *you've* got to do is walk back down your path and push it through your door," the girl retorted, staring at me with beady eyes.

"Fascinating as this conversation is"—Geena yawned—"we have to get a move on or we'll be late."

It was her turn to be given the evil eye by Tank Girl, who rolled the newspaper up into a tight cylinder and marched over to the gate.

I smiled to myself. You just had to be firm and stand your ground in this kind of situation.

What happened next was that the girl grabbed me by my school sweater and shoved the newspaper down the sweater's V-neck. Then she jumped on her bike and rode off. It all happened so fast, I couldn't move. I just stood there with the *Daily Telegraph* sticking out of my sweater.

Naturally, Geena and Jazz rushed to my aid. No, what I *actually* mean is that they nearly died laughing.

"How childish," Geena said at last, wiping tears from her eyes. "But funny."

"She was about a hundred times bigger than you, Amber," Jazz pointed out. "She could have flattened you."

"Maybe." I stomped up the path and posted the newspaper through our door. "But I'm sure I can think of a suitable way to get my revenge on that big ugly lump. Brains over brawn, and all that."

"Yes, but you don't have either," Geena remarked.

"If that isn't childish," I said haughtily, "I don't know what is. Let's go."

We set off for school. Along the way, we soon discovered that Mrs. Macey wasn't the only person who knew "the secret." Mrs. Dhaliwal, the local marriage broker and busybody, passed by in her car. When she spotted us, she began waving and beeping the horn loudly.

"Don't worry!" she screeched through the open window. "I won't tell a soul! But it's wonderful news, isn't it?"

Even Mr. Attwal at the minimarket knew. He was another of Auntie's success stories. Once he'd bored his customers with tales of what his life could have been like. Now, thanks to Auntie, he was studying computer technology and learning Italian, and boring them with progress updates. As we passed by the shop, he was serving someone, but he began dancing up and down excitedly and giving us thumbs-up signs.

"This is ridiculous." Jazz scowled as we walked on. "How can Mr. Attwal *possibly* know?"

"Didn't Auntie pop into the shop for some saag last night?" Geena said.

"Well, really!" Jazz was disgusted. "If adults can't keep a secret, how do they expect us to?"

"I still think we should keep quiet," I said. "If it can't be traced back to us, we can't get blamed."

"Keep quiet about what?" said Kim, who had just come up behind me.

What do you need to know about Kimberley Henderson? Kim is my friend, but she's also a major pain in the butt. She's another of Auntie's little projects.

BA (before Auntie), Kim was quiet and shy and wouldn't say boo to a mouse, let alone a goose.

PA (post-Auntie), she's becoming more assertive—

some would say obnoxious—by the day. I can't tell her what to do anymore. Now, is that a bad thing or is that a bad thing?

"Nothing." I telegraphed a warning to Geena and Jazz with my eyebrows.

"Of course it's *something*," Kim said spiritedly. "If it was nothing, you wouldn't have to keep quiet about it. And your eyebrows wouldn't be going up and down like they're on strings."

"Kim," I said, "when are you going to learn that there's a very thin line between being assertive and being annoying?"

"We can't tell you, anyway," Jazz chimed in.

"OK, let me guess." Kim stroked her chin, looking thoughtful. "You don't seem worried, so it can't be bad news. It must be something good. Is it a party? A new baby? A wedding? *Oh!*" Her eyes grew round as marbles. "Auntie and Mr. Arora are getting married!"

"Shhh!" I clapped my hand over Kim's mouth. "Do you want the whole town to know?"

"I think they already do," Jazz said.

"So it *is* true!" Kim spluttered, slapping my hand away. "I can't *believe* you weren't going to tell me!"

"Auntie told us not to," I said.

"Oh, like you three would take any notice of that!" scoffed Kim, very rudely, I thought.

"Actually, I find your tone quite offensive, Kim," Geena said. "We really haven't told anybody."

"See?" Jazz moaned. "I told you we were going to get blamed, whatever."

"Oh, this is great." Kim clasped her hands ecstatically. "I'm so happy! When's the wedding? Can I borrow a salwar kameez, Amber?"

"Who said you're invited?" I replied.

"I'd better be," Kim said, "or I'll want to know why not."

"Kim," I sighed as we reached the school gates, "don't you ever long for the days when you were quiet and sweet and shy?"

"Not at all," replied Kim, smiling widely. "This is so much more fun."

"Isn't this wonderful?" Jazz gazed reverently up at the new school building, a marvel of light, glass and sparkling paintwork. "No more bits of plaster in our hair while we're doing French conversation."

"It's a shame, in a way," I remarked, glancing at the old, tumbledown Coppergate School across the road, which was now being demolished. "The end of an era. A bit like us and Auntie."

"Hardly an era," Geena pointed out. "It's hardly been even a year."

"Oh!" Kim clapped a hand to her mouth. "I just realized—Auntie will be moving out, now she's getting married."

"What's that about your auntie?"

Chelsea Dixon and Sharelle Alexander, two of my friends, were hovering behind us, ears flapping. How they could overhear anything above the noise in the playground was a mystery, but nevertheless they were staring at us with eager faces.

"Auntie?" I shot Kim a warning look. "Oh, nothing."

"I thought you said she was getting married," Chelsea said accusingly.

"No, not married," said Geena. "*Carried.*"

"Carried?" Chelsea and Sharelle repeated suspiciously.

"Yes," Geena replied. "As in—er—carried away."

"Oh, that is so lame," Jazz muttered.

We all smiled brightly at Chelsea and Sharelle, who still looked suspicious. Everyone at school knew about Mr. Arora and Auntie's romance. They were following it with the kind of avid interest normally accorded to celebrity love affairs. If they even got a hint of the wedding, there would be an uproar.

Rescue was at hand from a most unlikely source.

"No footballs near the windows! And keep off the grass! It's for looking at, not walking on. Put your litter in the bins! No spitting!"

Mr. Grimwade was striding round the playground, yelling. He seemed rounder than ever, puffed up with importance at being made deputy head. He also seemed to have appointed himself custodian of the new school building. He glared at a Year 10 boy who'd dared to rest his elbow on a windowsill, and then homed in on us. He stopped frowning and started beaming.

"Ah, girls! Welcome back."

"Thank you, sir," I replied, wondering why he'd switched from stern to jolly mode. It wasn't long before I found out.

"Now, I'm not going to say a word," Mr. Grimwade said cheerily. "Not a word. I know it's meant to be a secret, and we respect that. But may I just say how pleased we all are for Mr. Arora. A wonderful woman, your aunt."

"Thank you," I said. And that was that. He might as well have announced it through a loudspeaker.

Mr. Grimwade bounced off to search out and destroy more disrespecters of school property. Meanwhile, Chelsea and Sharelle turned on me savagely.

"You utter scumbag, Ambajit Dhillon!" Chelsea shouted. "Your auntie *is* getting married!"

"To Mr. Arora," added Sharelle. "And you weren't going to tell us. How mean is that?"

"The Dhillons' auntie and Mr. Arora are getting married!" screeched a couple of Year 7 girls, and so it went on.

We stood there helplessly as the news filtered round the playground at speed, like a game of Chinese Whispers. It all got very emotional and one or two girls actually burst into tears. Mr. Arora was very popular, and many girls were in love with him. His new Year 8 class even decided to brave Mr. Grimwade and make an illegal dash into school before the bell, to paint a congratulations banner.

"Well, that's definitely let the cat right out of the bag," said Geena five minutes later. There couldn't have been a person in the packed playground who hadn't heard the news. "At least we don't have to pretend anymore."

"I'm exhausted," Jazz complained, "and school hasn't even started yet." She took off her jacket and drew interested looks from a group of boys.

"You don't have to keep sticking them out like that," I grumbled. "We're not blind."

"Oh, are they real?" Kim asked. "I thought she'd bought a padded bra."

"Some of us don't need to," Jazz said smugly.

"Well, I don't know why I'm hanging around with you lower-school losers," Geena remarked with a yawn. "So, see you later." She was about to stroll away when she stopped, suspended in midstep. "My God. Who is *that*?"

We turned to stare.

There was a boy coming through the gates. Tall, slim, tanned, hair bleached blond. Nice-looking. Better than nice. You could almost say handsome.

We knew every boy in the school. We had them filed, listed and scorecarded. We had them rated on a scale from one to ten. This boy wasn't one of them.

Or was he?

"Oh, I do not believe it," Jazz said faintly. "That is George Botley."

"*George Botley?*" Geena and Kim shrieked.

I couldn't say anything. I was too astonished.

George Botley? My short, verging-on-the-plump, pale-faced, mousy, annoying little admirer of the last eight years? No. It could not be possible.

"It *is*," Jazz insisted.

I looked more closely. The boy was coming toward

us. It *was* George. Apparently he'd had a body transplant in the past six weeks.

"Hey, Amber," he said casually. "How are you doing?"

A voice transplant too, by the sound of it. What had happened to his weedy, whiny, annoying voice? Where had these deep, manly tones come from?

We stood, mouths agape, as George sauntered past. I was astounded to see that he was already collecting a little gang of giggling females, who were trailing after him.

"Well!" Jazz looked gleeful. "How about that, Amber? I bet you wish you'd been nicer to him."

"Do you really think I'm that shallow?" I replied, trying to gather together the pieces of my shattered dignity.

"Why, yes," said Geena. "You missed out there, Amber."

"I think he still likes you," Kim said loyally.

"Oh, really." I yawned. I wasn't pretending. I honestly didn't care about George Botley one way or the other. No, *honestly*. "Like it matters."

"If he asked you out, would you go?" Kim persisted.

"Kim, boys are a waste of time for us," I replied. "Dad would never agree. His policy is to arrange the wedding first, then think about letting us date."

"Not that we've actually *tested* that policy," Geena remarked thoughtfully. "It might be worth a go."

"No chance." I scowled. "Boys mean trouble. Can

you imagine Auntie asking them if their intentions are honorable?"

At that moment I happened to glance across the playground. Someone else was coming through the gates. *Wow*.

My knees wobbled, then sagged. My heart began to flutter. I actually felt myself salivating, as if I'd just laid eyes on a delicious dessert.

And in a way, I had. Now this was a *boy*. If George was acceptable, this boy was unforgettable. Oh, he was lovely. Black hair artfully spiked around his beautiful face, deep brown, almost black, eyes. He wore his uniform like casual clothes, seeming utterly at home in it. And he was walking into our playground. It was as if Brad Pitt had just appeared, wearing a Coppergate uniform.

A ripple of female interest surged round the playground like a wave. The metamorphosis of George Botley from squat little caterpillar to reasonably attractive butterfly was completely forgotten.

"Oh!" said Kim faintly. "He must be a new boy. He's very good-looking, isn't he?"

"Good-looking?" Geena repeated, her eyes out on stalks. "Yes, you could say that."

"I'm in love," Jazz wailed. "Who *is* he?"

"Hands off," I instructed, my eyes glued to this vision on long legs. "I saw him first."

The bell rang as we watched the boy's every movement across the playground. Snake hips swaying, he disappeared through the upper-school entrance.

"Aha!" Geena said with delight. "He's in the upper school. He might even be in my class! Bye-bye, losers." And she took off at speed.

"How sickening," I grumbled as we shuffled our way over to the lower-school doors. "Trust Geena to get in there first."

"Watch out, Amber." Jazz linked arms with her friend Shweta King. "George'll be getting jealous."

"Oh, like he cares."

Nevertheless, I sneaked a glance at George. He was strolling into school, chatting happily with Chelsea and Sharelle. He did not look back.

"It's OK," Kim said. "I don't think he noticed."

I glared at her.

"Are you wearing a padded bra, Jazz?" Shweta inquired.

"No," Jazz snapped, stalking off down the Year 8 corridor.

Kim and I made our way to our new classroom. It was a revelation to see clean paintwork and lights that worked and coat hooks that weren't falling off the walls. George Botley was standing outside, now talking to Rebecca Hayward and Jasmine Cooper, but I wasn't one bit bothered. I'd just seen a vision of beauty that made George Botley pale in comparison.

"Where do you want us to sit, Mr. Hernandez?" Kim asked our new homeroom teacher. With his wiry black Medusa-like curls and retro dress sense, Mr. Hernandez was a legend throughout the school.

"On a chair," Mr. Hernandez replied absently. His

desk was already covered in books and folders, and he was searching through them rather halfheartedly. "Amber, have you stolen my register?"

"I believe you're sitting on it, sir," I replied.

"So I am." Mr. Hernandez stood up and whipped the register out from underneath him. "Have a gold star."

"You're too kind, sir."

I followed Kim across the room to sit with Chelsea and Sharelle. I have to say, they didn't look particularly welcoming.

"Oh, look," Chelsea said snootily, "it's our so-called mate, Amber."

"You mean the one who always tells us *everything*," twittered Sharelle with a sanctimonious glare.

"Give me a break," I groaned, sliding into a spare chair. "Besides, if we're talking about hypocrites . . ."

"I don't know who you could possibly mean," Chelsea said, very unconvincingly.

"Of course you do," I said. "I saw the two of you flirting with George Botley on the way in. When I think of all the times you've made fun because he's got a thing about me—"

"We weren't *flirting*," Sharelle said with an attempt at dignity. "We were just chatting. He told us he spent the summer working on his uncle's farm."

"Nice try," I said, "but your eyelashes were fluttering hard enough to power the national grid."

Chelsea and Sharelle blushed rosily.

"Well, what do you care?" Chelsea demanded. "You never liked him anyway."

"And it looks like he'll leave you alone from now on, Amber," Kim pointed out helpfully. "He's got so many girls after him."

We glanced at George. Last year he'd trampled half the class underfoot to try to get a seat just behind me. Now he was sitting on the other side of the room, and Marcia Grant had bagged the chair next to him. She'd had to elbow Victoria Kwame out of the way to get it.

"Good," I replied coolly. "I'm very happy for him."

Chelsea and Sharelle smirked. Kim frowned. I was seriously annoyed. I simply could not understand why nobody believed me.

A welcome diversion occurred when the door opened and Mr. Arora walked in. The class erupted into cheers and whoops, and George Botley yelled, "Nice one, sir!"

Mr. Arora turned pink. Trying not to smile, he ushered in a tall, lumpy-looking girl with a skinhead haircut.

"Oh, my God," I muttered.

Kim looked puzzled. "What is it?"

I shook my head. Geena got Golden Boy, and my class got Tank Girl. Isn't that just my luck.

"Nine J, *please*." Looking highly embarrassed, Mr. Arora held up his hand.

"Don't worry," Mr. Hernandez whispered loudly to him. "Your secret's safe with me."

The rest of the class chuckled. I didn't. I was fixing the new girl with a stony stare to remind her that I hadn't forgotten about the *Daily Telegraph* she'd shoved down my sweater. A spark of recognition flared in her eyes. Then she grinned. Yes. She *grinned.* Can you believe it? How rude.

Mr. Arora cleared his throat several times. "I'm pleased to welcome Kirandeep Kohli to the lower school," he said briskly. "She's going to be joining this class, and I hope you'll all make her feel very welcome. But I'm going to ask one particular person to keep an eye out for her and help her to settle in. . . ."

Oh no. Please. No.

I sank down in my chair and hid behind Kim.

"Amber?"

By this time I was practically under the table. Sulkily I hauled myself upright. "Yes, sir?"

"I'd like you to look after Kirandeep," Mr. Arora said, smiling at me. "Or Kiran, as she prefers to be called. I know you'll do a good job."

"She can sit here, next to Amber," Kim said assertively, moving to the next chair.

"Oh, thank you," I said, but my sarcasm went over everyone's head, except possibly Kiran's. She dragged her heavy rucksack across the room, looking as pleased as I felt.

"Do sit down," I said silkily. "*Aaaargh!*"

"Sorry." Kiran heaved her bag off my foot. "I didn't mean to drop it on you. It was an accident."

"Really?" I said through gritted teeth, massaging my throbbing toes.

"Oh, yes," Kiran replied cheerfully. And she had the nerve—the *nerve*—to grin at me.

There was no doubt that this was war.

chapter 3

"**K**iran delivers your newspapers?" Kim beamed at me as we lined up for assembly. "So you already know each other. Isn't that great?" Her smile faltered a little as she took a look at my face. If I were a cartoon character, I'd have had steam coming out of my ears. "Well, isn't it?"

"No, Kim," I assured her. "No, it is *not* great."

I took a quick look over my shoulder. By leaping out of my seat at the first peal of the bell, dodging round Chelsea and Sharelle and sprinting to the door, I'd got away from Kiran and made it to the front of the line. She was stuck near the back.

Kim was looking bewildered. "Why not?" she asked.

"Because a rather embarrassing incident occurred

this morning," I replied. "And before you ask, I don't want to go into details."

Mr. Hernandez wandered over to us. "Amber, did I just experience a time warp, or did Mr. Arora ask you to look after Kirandeep not five minutes ago?"

"He did, sir," I said, "but I didn't think I needed to hold her hand all the way to the assembly hall."

"Then I suggest you take your duties more seriously," Mr. Hernandez said sternly. "Go to the end of the line."

Fuming, I stepped out of the queue and went to the back to join Kiran. Loyally, Kim followed me.

"Oh, hello," said Kiran in a very offensive tone. "I thought you were trying to avoid me."

"I was," I replied.

"Well, you'd better try harder next time," she retorted.

"Oh, that's not going to help anyone, now, is it?" Kim said sensibly. "Why don't you try to be friends?"

We both stared savagely at her.

"All right"—Kim changed tack in a hurry—"maybe not *friends*. But you could be polite to one another."

"Polite people don't go around sticking newspapers down other people's sweaters," I replied.

Kiran grinned. Shockingly, Kim did too, until I gave her a look. We marched off to the assembly hall in angry silence.

Mr. Hernandez was always late, so we were last to arrive. The other classes had left a narrow gap in the middle of the enormous hall for us to squeeze into.

While we were inching our way into position, I took a good look round. The lower school had to sit on the floor, but the upper school had chairs. There was Geena, looking very smug, with an aren't-I-lucky-I-get-to-sit-on-a-chair-now face. Her eyes almost fell out of her head when she saw Kiran next to me. Jazz had turned round and noticed too, and both of them were smirking away.

I wasn't interested in their childish reaction, though. While we waited for Mr. Morgan, the head teacher, I twisted round to locate the delightful new boy. There he was, sprawled casually on a chair at the end of a row, looking as if he owned the place. He wasn't in Geena's class, although he was in the same year. Oh, he really did have everything, I thought dreamily, feasting my eyes. Looks, class, style—

"*Oof!*"

"Why don't you sit still?" Kiran snapped. She was so big, she'd taken up half of my tiny bit of space, and to add insult to injury, she'd just stuck her elbow in my ear.

"Well, if you weren't such a big lump, we'd all have a bit more room!" I retorted.

It was very unfortunate for me that, about a second before I spoke, Mr. Morgan had walked into the hall: you could have heard a pin drop in the sudden silence. Well, you might have heard a pin drop if I hadn't been speaking at pretty much the top of my voice.

"Ambajit Dhillon!" Mr. Morgan said coldly, peering at me over his half-moon glasses. "You will go and sit by your teacher. Immediately."

Oh dear. Somehow I managed to climb to my feet in a space the size of a envelope and make my way down the row to Mr. Hernandez. I was hot and cold all over with embarrassment.

Mr. Hernandez shook his head sadly and pointed at a patch of floor right next to his chair. "Not a very favorable start to the new term, is it, Amber?" he said.

I kept my head down for the rest of assembly. There was only one more slightly embarrassing moment when Mr. Morgan extended "a warm welcome to all our new pupils," and everyone turned to stare accusingly at me. Other than that, I was just mortified and humiliated. So, nothing too awful.

"Amber, correct me if I'm wrong," said Mr. Hernandez as he led the way back to class after assembly, "but I sense a feeling of hostility between you and our new girl."

"Oh, do you think so, sir?" I muttered bitterly.

"I do." Mr. Hernandez stared hard at me. "And it would be a big mistake to let it get out of hand. After all, Mr. Arora did specifically request that you help Kiran settle in."

"Yes, sir," I said in a dismal voice. What he meant was that I was stuck with her.

"It wasn't really Kiran's fault," Kim said cautiously as we collected our books for the first lesson.

"Are you saying it was mine?" I growled.

"No," Kim said quickly. "Well, maybe if you hadn't spoken quite so loudly—"

"It was all her fault for being so big and clumsy," I said in a five-year-old's voice. "It's not fair."

Kiran was at the front of the classroom talking to Mr. Hernandez. I longed to flounce out of the room without her, but I wasn't quite brave enough. If I had done, Mr. Hernandez would have told Mr. Arora, and Mr. Arora would have told Auntie, and oh, there would have been far too many consequences. I was slowly beginning to realize that maybe Mr. Arora marrying Auntie wasn't going to be all sunshine and roses.

"First lesson is English, right?" Kiran came over to us, timetable in hand. She and I had almost exactly the same timetable, so I would be responsible for her practically all day, every day. Hurrah.

"Room sixteen, with Mrs. Holland," replied Kim. I did not speak.

Kiran raised her eyebrows. "Not talking to me?" she inquired. "Well, maybe that's a good thing after what happened in assembly."

"This way," I said coldly, turning to the door. As far as I was concerned, my duties only extended to getting Kiran to the right classroom for the right lesson at the right time. I didn't have to spend every waking moment with her.

Mrs. Holland, however, had other ideas.

"Now, Kiran, you'll want to sit with Amber," she said as soon as we set foot in room sixteen. "You can have these seats right here."

Kiran and I both glared at her.

"I don't mind sitting on my own," muttered Kiran, much to my delight.

"So can I sit with Kim?" I asked.

Mrs. Holland looked thunderous. "Well, really, Amber, I'm surprised at you!"

"Me?" I spluttered. "What have *I* done?"

Rolling her eyes, Mrs. Holland pointed at the two seats in front of her. Looking glum, Kiran and I sat down next to each other.

"We're reading Shakespeare's *Julius Caesar* this term," Mrs. Holland explained as Kim and Chelsea handed the books out. "Amber, will you take the part of Caesar?"

"Is he the one who gets murdered?" Kiran asked. "Good casting."

I could not think of anything witty to say in reply— I know, unusual for me, wasn't it?—so I contented myself with elbowing Kiran's pencil case off the table when she wasn't looking. Childish, I guess. But it made me feel better.

I couldn't get away from Kiran all morning. At every lesson it was the same: *You'll want to sit by Amber, Kiran. Is Amber looking after you, Kiran? Amber will help you, Kiran. Just ask Amber, Kiran.* I was beginning to wonder if I was the victim of a teacher conspiracy.

"I don't get it," I complained to Kim. The last lesson of the morning was chemistry, and we were on our way to the science lab. "I mean . . ." I checked over my shoulder to make sure Kiran wasn't behind us. She'd disappeared into the girls' lavatories without a word to me or Kim. "*Why* are the teachers so worried about her settling in? She's big enough and ugly enough to look after herself."

"Oh, hello," said Geena, who was waiting outside the IT room with the rest of her class. "After that display in assembly this morning, Amber, I'm thinking of disowning you."

"It wasn't my fault," I grumbled. "It was Kiran."

"Mr. Arora's asked Amber to look after her," Kim added.

Geena began to chuckle. "Really? How amusing."

"Oh, never mind her," I said impatiently. "What details do you have on the delicious new boy?"

"Unfortunately, not much," Geena sighed. "He's not in my class, he's in Ten K. All I've got at the moment is that his name's Ragbir Gill, but he's known as Rocky."

"Amber!" Jazz was barreling her way down the corridor toward us, skidding on the highly polished wooden floor. "What was all *that* about in assembly this morning? And was that *really* the new papergirl?"

"I'm afraid so," I replied. "But don't worry. I'll soon show her what's what. She might be big and ugly, but I told you before—brains over brawn every time."

Jazz's gaze had shifted to a point beyond my shoulder. Geena and everyone in her IT class were staring in the same direction.

"She's behind me, isn't she?" I said.

Thirty-two people nodded. Slowly I turned round and came nose to nose with Kiran. However, we were only nose to nose because she was bending down quite a long way.

"So you're going to show me what's what, are you?" Kiran inquired in a not-at-all-friendly manner.

"Well." I cleared my throat. Took a step backward. Slipped on the polished floor.

I went over backward like a skittle in a bowling alley. I landed with a thump on my bottom, and my legs flew up in the air. There were a few wolf whistles, which turned to jeers as everyone got a first-class view of my big, sensible white school pants (Auntie's choice, not mine).

Only one person—someone who happened to be walking along the corridor toward me—put out a hand to help me up.

"Hello," said Ragbir Gill, known as Rocky, giving me a smile that could melt chocolate at twenty paces. "I don't think we've met."

"But Amber, we can't leave Kiran on her own," Kim twittered anxiously. "We ought to at least make sure she knows she goes to lunch now, or she'll miss the last lower-school sitting."

"After what she did to me?" I said bitterly, following her out of the canteen. "Just an hour ago I ended up flat on the floor, giving the most gorgeous boy in the school a good view of my knickers."

"Some people might think that's not necessarily a

bad thing," Kim said, attempting to be a woman of the world.

"I prefer to be a bit less obvious, thank you," I retorted, feeling a hot tide of embarrassment washing over me yet again. "Now that I've managed to sneak away from her, I want to enjoy the rest of the lunch hour in peace."

No hope of that. We were no sooner back in the playground than Jazz detached herself from her gang of mates and rushed over. Even Geena, who was trying to look all cool and upper-schoolish, couldn't resist the opportunity to come and join us.

"Everyone's talking about you, Amber," Jazz said gleefully. "You're getting a reputation."

"Yes," Geena said with a grin, "some of the girls are saying that flashing your knickers at a guy to get his attention is a bit much."

"Oh, shut up," I snapped. "You know it was an accident."

"Where's your little friend?" Geena asked, looking around.

"If you mean Kirandeep Kohli," I muttered, "we gave her the slip and went to lunch without her."

"I still think we should have waited for her," Kim said uneasily.

"Jazz, are you all right?" asked Geena with a frown.

Jazz was patting her hair, pulling down her school sweatshirt, hitching her skirt up higher and generally fidgeting about like a jumping bean.

"It's him!" she hissed. "And he's coming this way!"

Ragbir Gill, alias Rocky, was indeed walking purposefully in our direction.

I ran my fingers quickly through my hair and hoped I wasn't blushing. Or drooling.

"Hi." Rocky stopped in front of us, but he was looking at me. At *me*! "It's Amber, isn't it?"

"Yes," I blurted out in a voice two octaves higher than normal.

"I just wanted to see if you were OK." Rocky smiled at me, and I felt myself floating up to heaven on a silver cloud surrounded by angels. "That was quite a tumble you took."

I tried to look pale and fragile. "Oh, I'm fine, really—"

"Don't worry about Amber," Geena broke in. "She's as tough as old boots." She elbowed me aside and gave him a dazzling smile. "I'm Geena, her sister. I'm in Year Ten, same as you."

"And I'm Jazz, her other sister." Jazz jostled forward, pushing me out of the way and stepping on my toes in the process.

"You're not a sister too, are you?" Rocky laughed, turning to Kim.

"No, I'm a Kim," Kim burbled, completely mesmerized. "I mean, I'm just a friend."

"Nice to meet you all." Rocky raised a hand. "See you around, girls."

He strolled off, and we turned on each other.

"Talk about desperate!" I eyeballed Geena and Jazz

furiously. "Why didn't you both just leap on him there and then?"

"You can talk," Geena sniffed. "Fluttering your eyelashes and trying to look all girly and wistful. It was sickening."

"You two are such losers." Jazz smirked. "He liked me best. I could tell."

"He came over to talk to *me*," I reminded her coldly. "Who do you think he liked best, Kim?"

"Himself, probably," Kim replied. "He's almost *too* good-looking, isn't he?"

We ignored her.

"Jazz is out of it, obviously," said Geena. "So it's between you and me, Amber."

"Excuse me for not just lying down and letting you walk all over me," Jazz retorted, "but exactly *why* am I out of it?"

Geena sighed loudly. "Oh, really, Jazz! You're far too young for him."

"I'm nearly twelve and a half," Jazz said indignantly. "That's practically thirteen. *And* I've got the biggest chest."

"That just shows how immature you are," I said loftily. "This is not about chest size."

"All right." Geena turned to me. "What do you bet he likes me best?"

"Oh, are you sure you're up for this?" I asked with a confident smile. "After all, you're going to lose."

"We'll see," said Geena. "Kim can make the final decision."

"No, thanks," Kim said firmly.

"Or we could just ask him," I suggested.

"Fine," Geena replied.

"Fine," I repeated.

We stared challengingly at each other.

"What are we betting?" Geena wanted to know.

I took a Snickers bar from my pocket and began to rip it open. "Slave for a day?" I suggested.

"Nice one," said Geena. "But I must warn you that when I win, I'll be making you do all sorts of unpleasant and humiliating tasks."

"Same here," I replied. We'd had slave-for-a-day bets before. Last time I lost, Geena had ordered me to cut her toenails.

"I'm in this too," said Jazz stubbornly. "Or are you scared of the competition?"

"Not at all," Geena snapped.

"Oh, let her join in," I said. "It'll shut her up."

"We ought to have a deadline." Geena frowned. "What about Auntie's wedding? That gives us until just before half-term."

"Done," Jazz and I agreed.

"I think you're all mad," Kim said, with rather too much assertion, frankly.

I grinned. Someone tapped me on the shoulder and I looked round. It was Kiran. Her face was red and this time it was *her* turn to have steam almost coming out of her ears.

"Yes?" I said coldly.

"Why didn't you tell me I had to go for lunch half

an hour ago?" Kiran demanded. "Now I've missed the sitting."

"Sorry," I said, trying not to smile. I actually felt a tiny bit guilty. But not much when I remembered my big white pants disaster.

"If you go and explain to the teacher on duty," Kim began, "I'm sure they'll let you in—"

Kiran did not answer. She leaned over, whipped the Snickers bar from my hand and walked off.

"You—you!" I spluttered. "Come back! That's stealing!"

"Go after her and take it by force, Amber," suggested Geena. "It's the only way."

Jazz roared with laughter while Kim looked worried.

"Not at all," I said with dignity. "I told you, brains over brawn. I'll sort Kirandeep Kohli out *my* way."

Sadly, I didn't yet know what "my way" was.

"So tell me, Amber." Mr. Arora drove out of the school car park at a snail's pace to avoid the embarrassment of flattening any of his pupils. "How are you getting on with Kiran?"

"What?" I said absently, not listening. Mr. Arora had rounded us up at the end of the afternoon and told us that Auntie had asked him to drive us home as soon as possible, as we'd all been invited to tea with his parents. I wasn't listening because I was keeping an eye on George Botley, who was having a laugh with a couple of girls from Geena's year.

"How are you getting on with Kiran?" Geena and Jazz repeated together as loudly as they possibly could, just to embarrass me.

"Oh." I shrugged. "You know."

"Not really," Mr. Arora said in an inquiring voice. "Do you think she's settling in well?"

"I'm sure she is," I mumbled uncomfortably.

"She certainly enjoyed her lunch today," Jazz chimed in. I gave her a look.

"Well, I know you'll do your best to help her, Amber," Mr. Arora went on. This, of course, had the instant effect of making me feel like a toad. "Maybe you could invite her over to your house sometime—"

"What!" I gasped, just about stopping myself from adding, *No way—never on this earth will I ever do that.*

Geena and Jazz were doing their best not to explode with laughter. They succeeded easily when Mr. Arora added, "Then Geena and Jazz could get to know Kiran too. In fact, I think it would be a great idea if all three of you did your best to make her feel welcome."

"So do I," I agreed, smiling at Geena and Jazz. They both lapsed into a sulky silence, which lasted until we reached our house.

Auntie was standing at the curb, helping Mrs. Macey into a cab. The driver slung a heavy suitcase into the boot, and the taxi pulled away as Mr. Arora drew to a halt.

"What's going on?" Jazz asked nosily as we climbed out of the car.

"I've finally managed to persuade Gloria to go and

visit her daughter in Southampton," replied Auntie. She was dressed for tea with Mr. Arora's parents in a pale pink suit embroidered with silver, and strappy silver sandals.

"You mean the one she hasn't spoken to for five years?" I asked. "Just because she's married to a black guy?"

Auntie nodded. "She's never even seen her two grandchildren," she said. "I've told her to bring them all to the wedding."

"Imagine not speaking to a close relative for five years," Geena remarked. "Although after what happened in assembly this morning, I can understand it completely."

"What happened in assembly this morning?" asked Auntie, onto the trail like a bloodhound.

"We don't really have time for this now," Mr. Arora broke in. I threw him a grateful look. "We'll see you in about half an hour."

He waved and drove off.

"Isn't that Mrs. Macey thing just *so* Auntie?" Geena said admiringly as we went into the house. "Here she is, with her wedding coming up, yet she still has time to go around interfering in other people's lives."

"I know," I replied. "It's a remarkable achievement."

We ran upstairs to get changed and fight over the bathroom with Dad, who'd come home early from work. Jazz started getting on my nerves, fussing about which outfit she was going to wear. I decided to take my revenge by locking her wardrobe and sticking the key down my bra. We ended up wrestling for supremacy on the bed.

"You know what," Jazz panted, trying to wriggle out of the headlock I'd got her in, "I'll be so-o-o glad when you move back into your own room."

"Oh!" I said. "I'd forgotten about that." Of course, when Auntie moved out, I'd get my bedroom back. That was one good thing.

Geena strolled in, looking deliciously cool in a violet silk skirt, matching short top and floaty chiffon wrap. "Aren't you two ready yet?"

Jazz snatched the key from the duvet, where it had fallen. "Amber's being very childish," she said, flouncing over to the wardrobe. "I hardly think that's going to impress Rocky Gill."

"Oh, and you think *you* will?" I scoffed.

"You can mock," Jazz replied snootily, whipping out an orange and gold suit with wide-legged trousers and a funky beaded scarf, "but I have a plan to win this bet."

"So do I," said Geena.

"And you think I don't?" I said quickly.

I didn't. But I was going to think of one very quickly.

"Girls, it's time to go." Dad popped his head round the door five minutes later. "You all look very nice." He sighed and shook his head. "You know, I really can't believe that my little sister's getting married."

"Dad, you're not going to cry, are you?" asked Geena.

Dad blinked. "Of course not," he said. "We have to

think about what we're going to do when your aunt moves out, though. I might hire a housekeeper."

"Someone to cook and clean?" Jazz's face lit up. "Excellent."

"And to look after the three of you."

"Dad!" Geena protested. "I'm fifteen in a couple of months. I really don't need a babysitter."

"We'll see," Dad said, and went out.

"We certainly will," Geena promised grimly. "I think we need to put a stop to that little idea, girls, wouldn't you say?"

"You bet," Jazz and I agreed.

We'd met Mr. Arora's parents before. They were lovely. His dad was very gentle and quiet, with a shock of white hair, and his mum was small and thin and always smiling. As we sat in their living room, she kept blessing us and thanking Guru Nanak, whose picture was on the wall, for bringing her such a good daughter-in-law.

"I thought our *beta* would never find a wife." She beamed as she handed round the plates of barfi, laddoo and gelabi for the fifth time. "I was beginning to despair of ever having any grandchildren."

The tips of Mr. Arora's ears turned pink, and Auntie looked pleased but embarrassed. The three of us were enjoying it all enormously, of course.

"The boy was married to his job," Mr. Arora (senior) added. He turned to Dad. "More whisky?" he asked, pouring it anyway.

44

"I'll drive home if you've had too much tea, Johnny," Auntie whispered.

"Our Jai was always such a good boy," Mrs. Arora went on, forcing a third samosa on Jazz. "He studied hard, never gave us a moment's trouble."

I decided it was time to stir things up a bit. Playfully, of course.

"Do you have any baby photos?" I asked. "We'd love to see them."

Auntie threw me a sour look. Mr. Arora (junior) gulped.

"Oh, come now, Amber," he said. "You're not really interested."

"We are," the three of us chorused. We were possibly motivated by a teeny-weeny desire for revenge at having Kirandeep Kohli so unceremoniously foisted on us.

Mrs. Arora looked thrilled. "Of course, we have hundreds!" she proclaimed with glee. "Wait one moment—"

Bang! We all jumped. Someone had just flung open the front door with a resounding crash. *Bang!* We all jumped again as it closed. *Thump! Thump! Thump!* We heard footsteps coming down the hall toward the living room.

"What the hell is going on?" Geena whispered in my ear.

I did not have time to reply before—*bang!*—the living room door was thrown open.

A woman in a pink sari stood there grinning widely at us. She was almost as broad as she was tall. She virtually filled the doorway.

Then, with a joyful shriek, she raced across the room, trampling my toes in the process, and hauled Auntie off her chair into a bone-crushing embrace. I have a confused memory of Auntie's feet not even touching the floor.

"We meet at last!" the woman roared. "Oh, how I've longed for this day!"

Auntie looked stunned and for once was speechless.

"Hello, Auntie-ji," Mr. Arora began.

"Ah, come here and give your old auntie a hug!" The woman turned to Mr. Arora, hauled *him* off his chair and pinned him to her large bosom.

"I hope we're not next," Jazz whispered.

Sadly, we were. Mr. Arora's auntie worked her way round the room like a boa constrictor, hugging the life out of each of us and leaving us half dead on the sofa.

"Now!" She stood in the center of the room, hands on her hips. "Tell me what wedding arrangements have been made so far."

"Well, not many," Mrs. Arora began timidly.

Auntie-ji held up a large, square hand. "Then you can leave it all to me," she proclaimed happily. "I'm going to take everything off your hands."

She leaned over and pinched Auntie's cheek. I think it was meant to be affectionate, but it seemed to hurt. Auntie had been speechless for the past five minutes, which was probably a world record.

"Oh, this is going to be so much fun," I whispered to Geena and Jazz. "Now Auntie's got an interfering auntie too!"

chapter 4

"I don't like lying," Kim said, frowning. "It shows a lack of integrity."

"Oh, please," I retorted. "You can't even spell *integrity*. And if you're that bothered, why don't you go to the library right now? Then it won't be a lie, will it?"

It was two days after tea with the Aroras. Things were not going well on any fronts. Auntie still hadn't recovered from her encounter with Mr. Arora's auntie. Apparently she was legendary amongst the Arora family for sticking her nose in and having the hide of an elephant when it came to listening to hints. Auntie-ji had elaborate, expensive and outrageous ideas for every aspect of this wedding, from the reception venue to Auntie's shoes. Auntie had been overheard telling Mr. Arora that he was going to have to put his foot down and stop her from interfering so much. Mr. Arora had looked quite ill.

More importantly, I hadn't had any chance to get to know Rocky better. In fact, I'd hardly seen him. My only consolation was that Geena and Jazz didn't seem to be getting on that well either. Geena's only claim to fame was that she'd stood behind him in assembly the day before, and she could confidently state that he had a lovely neck.

Mr. Arora was still going on at me about looking after Kiran Kohli, who did not improve on closer acquaintance. Luckily we seemed to have reached some sort of truce. A silent one. We didn't speak to each other unless there was a teacher watching.

So now my idea was this: I had to get Rocky on his own, without my two ugly sisters around. The only possible time was before school. I'd noticed that Rocky had arrived ahead of us the previous day, so I was hoping he would do the same this morning. And somehow I had to lose Geena and Jazz along the way.

Of course, this simple plan involved an elaborate ruse on the scale of plotting to steal the Crown Jewels. First, I had to tell Auntie that I was going into school early because Kim and I had to go to the library to finish a project we were doing together. I added Kim into the mix because I thought it sounded more authentic. But then, tiresomely, I had to tell Kim because Auntie was quite capable of ringing her to check that this was true. It's *so* inconvenient having inquisitive relatives.

Second, I knew that Geena and Jazz would smell a big fat rat if they found out I was going into school early. And I couldn't ask Auntie not to mention it because she'd want to know why not. So I just had to hope she didn't say anything until after I'd gone. That was always unlikely where Auntie was concerned, but luckily for me she was out for most of the evening with Mr. Arora. All that was left was for me to hide my school uniform in the airing cupboard, wake myself up early without an alarm, sneak out of bed without rousing Jazz, wash and dress without waking Geena, and tiptoe out of the house. Easy, really.

"It would still be a lie, even if I went to the library now," Kim replied doggedly. "It would be a lie in retrospect."

"Have you swallowed a dictionary?" I jeered, arranging my fringe so that it fell casually over one eye. "Anyway, you might as well go to the library as anywhere else. I need you to push off"—my face brightened as Rocky sauntered through the gates— "like, right now."

"Are you sure you don't want me to stay?" asked Kim. "You might make a fool of yourself without me to help."

I sent her packing with a look. Then I dropped my bag at my feet, hitched my school skirt a little higher and smiled sweetly.

Rocky came over to me. The sunlight glinted on his jet-black hair, and I felt my heart quiver and my knees weaken.

"Fancy a Polo mint?" he asked, holding out the tube.

I hate Polos. Of course, I took one. If he'd offered me a pebble, I'd have eaten it.

"How're you doing?" he asked.

"Fine. What about you? How are you settling in?" My voice sounded fluttery, so I took a deep breath.

Rocky shrugged. "Schools are all the same, aren't they?" he drawled. "Same old crap."

"Absolutely," I agreed breathlessly, hanging on his every wonderful word.

Rocky glanced over his shoulder. "Your sisters not around?"

Curses! Did that mean he liked one of them better than me?

"No," I said quickly. "Jazz likes to watch cartoons in the morning before she comes to school. Well, she *is* only twelve. And Geena has to see the doctor this morning. About her rash."

"Rash?" Rocky repeated.

"Yes," I replied. "Her skin's been peeling off for weeks. Apparently it's very contagious."

Rocky looked surprised. "I hadn't noticed."

"Oh, it's only on her arms and legs," I said cheerfully. "But it might be best to keep your distance."

"I got ya." Rocky pointed a finger at me. "See you later?"

"Yes," I said eagerly, just about stopping myself from adding *please*. "Maybe we could meet up at lunchtime?"

Rocky nodded lazily, and off he strolled to join a

bunch of Year 10 boys who were kicking a football about.

"Yes!" I mentally punched the air. Then I muttered, "Oh dear."

Geena and Jazz were standing just inside the gates, glaring at me. Their looks were bitter.

"Oh, so *this* is where the library is, is it?" Jazz remarked with heavy sarcasm as she came toward me. "I thought it was *inside* the school."

"Really, Amber!" said Geena sternly. "I didn't think you could stoop so low."

"Nonsense," I said. "All's fair in love and war."

"Oh, so you've been found out." Kim appeared, clutching a library book. "Serves you right."

"I don't care," I said smugly. "It was worth it."

"What did you talk about?" Jazz asked, clearly bursting to hear everything. Geena was too, but she would have died before asking.

I tapped Jazz lightly on the nose. "Wouldn't you like to know?" I said jauntily.

The bell rang. Jazz was about to attack me, so you could say I was literally saved by the bell. I bounced into school feeling very cheerful, followed by Kim, who radiated disapproval from every pore.

"Hey, Georgie." I smiled at George Botley, who was hanging his jacket up. "How's it going?"

"OK." George smiled back. The improvement was tremendous, but sadly he still wasn't in the Golden Boy league. For a moment it looked as if he was going to come over. But then his path was blocked by Victoria Kwame, who grabbed his arm and started twittering about maths homework.

I shrugged and turned away. I had bigger fish to fry, anyway.

Kiran was already at our table, reading a history textbook. I could feel Mr. Hernandez's eyes boring two red-hot holes in my back as I went over to her. At least getting up early meant I hadn't run into her delivering newspapers.

"All right?" I said with as much of a fake smile as I could muster.

"Fine," she snapped, baring her teeth.

I shot a glance at Mr. Hernandez, resplendent in a purple Hawaiian shirt dotted with yellow tropical blooms. Our short exchange seemed to have satisfied him, and he opened the register.

Looking flustered, Kim joined us. "I can't find my *Julius Caesar* notes," she said. "I wondered if either of you had picked them up by mistake."

I rooted through my bag. "Not me." I glanced at Kiran. "Aren't you going to look too?" I demanded.

"In a minute," she snapped. She didn't even have the courtesy to raise her eyes from her book.

"You know, it really is an art to be this obnoxious," I said in a low voice. "Congratulations."

"It doesn't matter, Amber—" Kim began.

"Of course it does." I noticed Mr. Hernandez staring at us again, and pasted a smile to my face. "She can't talk to you like that."

"She wasn't talking to me," Kim replied. "She was talking to you."

Kiran glared, spotted Mr. Hernandez and gave us an artificial smile. "Why don't you two just shove off and leave me in peace?" she suggested through her teeth.

"You're a complete pain in the butt—you do know that, don't you?" I said with a savage grin.

"Glad to see you're all getting on so well, girls," called Mr. Hernandez.

"You should have asked Kiran nicely," Kim said as we went off to our first lesson—maths with Mr. Arora. "You were a bit rude. And you didn't need to stand up for me either."

"I've been doing it since we were five," I said. "You've never complained before."

"You just wanted to interfere," retorted Kim.

"Thanks for being such a good friend, Amber," I said pointedly. "No, really, Kim, don't mention it."

"I won't," Kim replied.

We stopped in the corridor before we reached Mr. Arora's classroom, and turned to look for Kiran. This was our new routine. Kiran would join us, and we'd go into the classrooms together, so that the teachers didn't have anything to moan about. Then at the end of the lesson we'd leave together and instantly go our separate ways. It was the only way to avoid attacking each other.

But I had more pressing problems on my mind than

Kiran. I had to plan my next move on Rocky Gill, as well as keep one step ahead of the others. . . .

"Jazz, what are you doing?" I asked with eyebrows raised.

It was lunchtime, and Kim and I were sharing a quiet moment and a Twix, when people began to laugh and point at the canteen. I looked to see what was so amusing and saw Jazz clinging to one of the canteen windowsills like a monkey.

"Trying to look through the window, of course," Jazz snapped, scrabbling for a nonexistent toehold. "Oh!" She collapsed feebly to the ground.

"This might sound like a silly question," I began, "but why are you so desperate to spy on kids eating their lunch?"

"The Year Tens are in there," Jazz replied, dusting off her black over-the-knee socks. "And Geena's somehow managed to nick a seat next to Rocky."

"What!"

I pushed Jazz out of the way, grabbed the windowsill and hauled myself up. As I was about thirty centimeters taller than she was, I had a good view.

Geena and Rocky were sitting at a table near the window, eating banoffee pie and custard. I couldn't hear anything, but I could tell that, in between bites, Geena was flirting relentlessly.

"What are they doing?" Jazz asked as I let go of the sill.

"Talking," I replied. "And Geena's coming on pretty strong. Has the girl got no shame?"

"It's so not fair," grumbled Jazz. "Geena's in the same year as Rocky, so she's got a much better chance of getting to know him than we have. We should have given her a handicap before we made the bet."

"Like what?" I asked.

"We could have made her wear an eye patch," Jazz muttered bitterly.

"I think you're all mad," said Kim. "Why don't you just forget this stupid bet?"

At that moment Rocky and Geena came out of the canteen, laughing together. They looked very, very cozy.

"What's that noise?" Kim asked.

"It's Jazz grinding her teeth," I replied. "She does it sometimes when she's annoyed."

Geena spotted us and tried to steer Rocky in the opposite direction, but Jazz and I were having none of it. We hurried after them, sliding ahead to cut them off at the corner.

"Oh, hello," said Geena unconvincingly. "I didn't notice you two."

"Obviously," I replied, "or you wouldn't have walked off in the opposite direction."

"Sorry," Geena sighed. "I'm so scatty these days. It must be the medication I'm taking. You know, for my terrible skin rash."

I tried very hard not to blush.

"What skin rash?" asked Kim.

"Well, amazingly, it's all gone!" Geena rolled up the sleeve of her white shirt. "See?"

"Let's hope your little problem clears up just as quickly, Amber," said Rocky solemnly.

"My little problem?" I repeated, bewildered.

"I know you don't like talking about it." Rocky lowered his voice. "But when you've had it lanced, bring a cushion to school to sit on. It's the only way."

Kim and Jazz started giggling hysterically.

"Geena," I said in a dignified manner, "a word with you. In private."

We edged a discreet distance away.

"Can I ask why you told Rocky I'd got a boil on my behind?" I demanded in a low voice.

"For the same reason you told him I'd got a contagious skin disease on my arms and legs," retorted Geena.

"Oh, that," I said dismissively. "It was just a joke."

"Exactly," Geena agreed. "And I was able to show him that it wasn't true. May I ask if you're going to do the same?"

I glared at her. "Oh, that's funny."

"All's fair in love and war," Geena reminded me. She glanced over my shoulder and frowned. "*What* is going on?"

I turned to see Jazz and Rocky standing close together and gazing into each other's eyes. Of course, Geena and I galloped over there immediately.

"Jazz says she's got something in her eye," Kim said dryly. "I offered to take a look, but she said no."

56

"I think it's all right now." Jazz peeped under her eyelashes at Rocky. She had one hand on his arm, the shameless hussy. "Thank you."

Geena and I were seriously annoyed. There was no saying what might have happened next if redheaded Karl Peterson, who was in Year 8, hadn't come over to us.

"Mr. Arora wants to see you," he said without preamble, "in his classroom right now."

"You heard him, Jazz," I said. "Mr. Arora wants to see you."

"No, all of you," Karl insisted. "Right now."

"Are you sure he said *all* of us?" asked Geena.

"*All* of you," Karl said. "Do you want me to write it down?"

"Don't be cheeky, you lower-school scumbag," Geena told him.

Karl shrugged and sauntered off.

"You'd better go, girls," Rocky drawled. "Catch you later."

"I think you three are making a big mistake," Kim said sternly as Rocky wandered away. "He's guessed what you're up to. And he thinks it's amusing."

"Oh, stop being so prim, Kim," Geena exclaimed. "This is just a bit of fun."

"Of course it is," I agreed as we went in search of Mr. Arora. "But really, Jazz! Pretending to have something in your eye. That's one of the oldest in the book."

"He fell for it, though," Jazz said with satisfaction. "And I got really close to him." She sighed. "He smells of pine and lemon."

"You make him sound like toilet cleaner," I snapped.

"You're just jealous," Jazz replied with deadly accuracy.

"He thinks you're a kid, Jasvinder," Geena said loftily.

"He doesn't!"

"Does!"

"Doesn't!"

"Oh, very mature," I said as they began hitting each other to make their point.

"Who asked you?" Geena retorted, giving me a shove. I reeled against Mr. Arora's door, unfortunately at exactly the same moment as he opened it.

"Are you all right, Amber?" he asked anxiously as I picked myself up off the floor.

"I'm fine, sir," I said through my teeth. Up until then, I'd been treating our bet as a jolly bit of fun. But from now on the gloves were definitely *off*.

"You wanted to see us, sir?" Geena said inquiringly.

Mr. Arora closed the classroom door behind us. "Yes. I have a question to ask you."

I thought it must be something to do with the wedding. Oh dear. How wrong I was.

Mr. Arora sat down at his desk and steepled his fingers together. "Where is Kiran?" he asked gravely.

"Who?" I blurted out.

Mistake. Of course I knew who Kiran *was*. I'd just forgotten about her, that's all.

"The papergirl," Jazz said helpfully. "The one who's in your class."

"Thank you," I mumbled. "I do know."

"Well, where is she?" Mr. Arora repeated.

I shrugged. I hadn't seen her since French conversation, just before lunch.

Mr. Arora was looking deeply pained. "There she is." He pointed out of the window. Kiran was sitting on her own on a bench in the playground, reading a magazine.

Jazz looked puzzled. "If you know where she is, then why are you asking us?"

Mr. Arora looked even more pained. "As you can see, she's on her own. And this is the second day I've seen her sitting on her own at lunchtime *and* break time." He turned reproachful, puppy-dog eyes on us. "I did ask you if you could help her settle in."

"It's not our fault," I said defensively. "She's not exactly the easiest person in the world to get along with." This was putting it as politely as I could.

Mr. Arora sighed. "I accept that. But if you could all try a little harder to make friends with her, I think she'd respond. Will you give it a go?"

We didn't say anything for a moment. I'm sure Geena and Jazz were having exactly the same thoughts as I was—which were that there was no way we'd be in this awkward position if Mr. Arora wasn't engaged to Auntie. However, I could just imagine the hassle Auntie would give us if we didn't do what he asked.

"We'll try," I said gloomily.

"This is ridiculous," Geena complained when we were a safe distance away from Mr. Arora's classroom. "Why do *we* have to be the ones to make an effort? If this girl hasn't made any friends yet, it's because nobody likes her."

"She looks like a thug too." Jazz shuddered melo-dramatically. "That hair."

"You know, technically Mr. Arora can't make me do anything," Geena said thoughtfully. "He's head of the lower school, and I'm in the upper school."

"Oh, I'd like to see you tell him that," Jazz sniggered. "Auntie would love it."

"I'm not scared of Auntie," retorted Geena.

"Of course you are," Jazz said. "We *all* are."

"This is your fault, Amber." Geena turned on me. "If you hadn't annoyed Kiran the first time you met, she might be a bit more pleasant."

"May I remind you that I was the one who had a newspaper stuffed down her sweater?" I snapped. "Look, we're missing the point here."

"Which is?" Jazz queried.

"Well, don't you think Mr. Arora and the other teachers are coming on a bit heavy?" I went on. "We've had new kids start at the school loads of times. And they don't usually have such a big fuss made of them."

Geena frowned. "You mean—there's something odd about Kiran?"

"That's exactly what I mean," I replied. "There's some sort of mystery. . . ." I thought for a moment. "I think I've got it."

"What?" Jazz asked eagerly.

"I reckon Kiran was a troublemaker at her last

school," I said slowly. "Maybe even a bully. And Mr. Arora's doing his best to stop her from going down that road again here."

Geena put her head on one side as she considered. "Actually, that makes perfect sense," she admitted.

"She *looks* scary," said Jazz. "Yes, I'll buy that."

"I suppose we'd better go and talk to her," I sighed as we went into the playground. "I wouldn't be surprised if Mr. Arora's watching us from his classroom window."

"If we could get her annoyed, she might thump one of us," said Jazz eagerly. "Then she'd be expelled, and we'd be rid of her forever."

"I nominate Amber," said Geena.

"Forget it," I said. "We're all in this together."

Kiran glanced up from her magazine as we approached. She looked totally underwhelmed to see us.

"Hi," I said in a jolly voice. "How's it going?"

"Go away," snapped Kiran. "I know you're only here because Mr. Arora sent you."

"Oh, that's nonsense," Geena blustered.

"I saw you in his classroom," she said coolly. "And he's watching us right now."

We all turned round just in time to see Mr. Arora dive out of sight behind a cupboard.

"Er—all right, I admit it," I muttered. "But at least we're *here*—"

"Excuse me," Jazz murmured, sidling away, "I need the bathroom."

"So why don't you try being a bit more pleasant?" I went on. "We might end up getting on better."

61

"Sorry," whispered Geena, backing away from me. "Something I've got to do."

"You think we could be friends?" Kiran asked with a fixed smile on her face.

"Well, maybe *friends* is a bit strong," I said cautiously. "How about distant acquaintances?"

"Speaking of friends"—Kiran's smirk was getting wider—"your sisters seem to be getting on awfully well with that boy."

"Which boy?" I roared, spinning round.

There was Rocky, and there were Geena and Jazz fluttering around him like flirtatious butterflies. How sneaky is that?

"Sorry," I threw over my shoulder at Kiran. "Something just came up."

"Don't worry," Kiran called after me sarcastically. "Tell Mr. Arora I'll be fine."

Call me an idiot (Jazz and Geena do, often), but I felt a *teeny* bit guilty as I charged over to elbow my way between Rocky and Geena. But why should I? If Kiran wasn't going to try to be friendly, then why should I?

"I see you're playing it cool with Rocky," Kim remarked as we headed into school a little later for afternoon lessons.

"I was only hanging on to his arm because I felt a bit faint," I said dismissively.

"I could tell that Jazz and Geena were concerned," Kim replied, "by the way they were trying to shove you aside."

I ignored her. "You know, this isn't getting me any-where," I said.

"Oh, good." Kim looked relieved. "Are you going to forget about this ridiculous bet, then?"

"I didn't mean that," I said. "I meant that my strategy to get Rocky to like me best isn't working."

Kim raised her eyebrows. "I didn't know you had a strategy."

"I was relying on my natural charm."

"Well, that was bound to be a mistake, wasn't it?"

I resisted the urge to put my hands round Kim's throat and squeeze. "I need to find out more information about him," I said thoughtfully. "Where he lives. What he likes doing at weekends. His hobbies."

"There was a bhangra CD sticking out of his bag," remarked Kim.

I stared at her. "Are you sure? I didn't notice."

"You were too busy fluttering and twittering around like a lovesick parrot," Kim replied. "Yes, I'm sure."

"Nice work, Sherlock." I grinned, slapping Kim heartily on the back. "That's just the kind of inside information I need."

The following day, Friday, started promisingly. This time I had a plan, and I laughed smugly and silently as I watched Geena and Jazz falling over themselves to impress Rocky before school. The obvious was no longer for me. I was going to be subtle. I was going to be cool. And I would win. *Yes*, he would be mine, all mine.

Break time was the appointed hour for me to put my plan into action. Before Miss Jackson had finished giving out German homework, I was sneaking my books into my bag. When the bell went, I leaped to my feet like a light-footed gazelle.

"Shall we—" Kim began.

But I never did hear what she was proposing. I whisked out of the classroom and into the playground to make my move, leaving Kim far behind me.

I was actually the first person out there, which has never happened to me before or since. But seconds later doors opened all round the building, and streams of other kids came pouring out.

I waited and watched. It was essential that Rocky come out before Geena and Jazz. Otherwise my plan would have to wait till another day.

Oh, joy. Here he was.

Now it was up to me. I fumbled in my bag and found my bhangra CD. We had quite a few of them lying around at home, and I'd chosen one by Punjabi MC.

I sidestepped my way casually over to Rocky. He didn't see me. Then I "accidentally" dropped the CD in his path, rather like a Victorian lady might have dropped a handkerchief in front of her admirer.

"Oh, silly me—" I began.

Of course, my plan was for Rocky to pick it up, say,

"Why, Amber, I didn't know you were into bhangra! You've got good taste as well as being stunningly beautiful," etc., etc.

It didn't work out at all like that. Oh, Rocky bent down to pick up the CD, yes he did. But at exactly that precise moment, George Botley dived in from the left to do the same. Their heads met with a resounding crack.

"George, you idiot!" I muttered.

"Ow!" George moaned, rubbing the side of his head.

"Are you all right, Rocky?" I asked anxiously.

"Yeah, I reckon so." Rocky shot George a poisonous stare. "You want to look where you're going, mate."

"You sure you're not concussed or something?" I went on, ignoring George, who wandered away, looking sheepish.

"I'm fine." Rocky checked out the CD, then handed it to me. "So you're into bhangra?"

"Why, yes," I said flirtatiously. "Isn't everyone?"

"I'm into bhangra fusion," Rocky replied. "Hip-hop and rap mainly. I write my own stuff, you know. I like to mix in a bit of reggae and sometimes a few Bollywood beats too."

"You do?" I breathed. Was there anything Golden Boy couldn't do?

"Yeah." Rocky was all lit up with enthusiasm. "I've got my own recording studio with decks and everything at home. My dad's helping me set it up in the flat over our garage."

65

"Where do you live?" I asked. This was the very information that might help me win the bet.

"We've just moved into Temple Avenue," Rocky replied.

Wow. Now I was impressed. You had to be quite seriously loaded to live in Temple Avenue. The whole of our street would fit into one back garden there.

"Someone told me that there's a fantastic music shop called Shanti's on the Broadway," Rocky went on. "Do you know it? I thought about checking it out tomorrow afternoon."

"Oh, I know it," I said. "I go myself most weekends." Which was almost true. I did pop in there occasionally. "Maybe I'll see you there?"

"You got it." Rocky pointed his finger at me. "I'll be there after lunch."

Oh, me too, I promised him silently as he strolled off. Even if it meant locking Geena and Jazz in the garden shed. Even if it meant tying Auntie to the cooker with a length of rope. I'd be there.

chapter 5

"I've got a big pile of dirty socks to be washed. By hand. My trainers need new Odor-Eaters. My hairbrush needs de-hairing, and I must have the hard skin on my feet removed." I sighed happily. "Oh, how I love having slaves."

"You're wasting your time with that list," Jazz called. She was sprawled on our bed, straightening her hair with ceramic irons. "I won't end up being your slave for a day. You and Geena will be *mine*."

I ignored her. "Oh, and my pet snake's tank needs cleaning out."

Jazz looked puzzled. "You don't have a pet snake."

"I know," I replied. "I'm thinking of getting one, just so you can clean it out."

"Hmm," Jazz said suspiciously. "You seem very confident that you're going to win this bet."

"Quietly confident, yes," I agreed, looking as innocent as I knew how. "I know that my charm and good looks and personality will carry the day."

"Just how insane *are* you?" Jazz inquired.

I prevented myself from smiling even just a little. Of course, Jazz and Geena could not know about my plan to meet Rocky that very afternoon at Shanti's music shop. I had prepared myself by putting on my new cropped jeans and pink T-shirt, with subtle makeup— just a touch of Pink Poodle lip gloss and mascara.

Geena put her head round our bedroom door. "Auntie's in a terrible mood," she whispered. "She's tearing Mr. Arora to bits downstairs."

"How could you possibly know that," I asked, "unless you were listening at the door?"

"I was just passing by, and the living room door happened to be ajar," Geena replied. "Oh, what the hell. Yes, I listened."

"Is it about Mr. Arora's auntie?" asked Jazz.

Geena nodded. "Her latest idea is that they hold the reception in the gardens of a stately home, and have peacocks wandering about. Oh, and she wants Mr. Arora to arrive at the gurdwara riding a white Arab stallion. With maybe a peacock or two there as well."

"That'll be fun, trying to ride a horse down the Broadway," I remarked.

"So Auntie's really mad," Jazz giggled. "Ooh, I want to hear."

68

She slid off the bed and headed for the door. Geena followed her downstairs, so I thought I might as well go too. We all felt a bit sorry for Auntie, really, but we couldn't help enjoying the fact that she'd found out what it was like to have an interfering relative. It was karma. Definitely.

"I'll end up tearing my hair out at this rate," Auntie sighed as we gathered at the bottom of the stairs to listen. "Is that what you want? A bald bride?"

"I'm sure you'd still look lovely," said Mr. Arora placatingly.

"*Seriously*, Jai." Auntie sounded very annoyed. "You're going to have to tell her, as politely as you can, that Johnny and your parents are making the final decision on all the arrangements."

"Um . . ." Mr. Arora, on the other hand, sounded depressed. "It's not quite as easy as that, Susie. She means well, you know."

"I know," Auntie agreed. "Unfortunately, that doesn't really help."

"It's just that she hasn't got any family of her own to fuss over," Mr. Arora said apologetically. "My uncle died a few years ago, and her son moved to the USA."

"Presumably because there aren't any direct flights to the moon yet," Auntie muttered.

"He didn't do it to get away from her." Mr. Arora sounded a little annoyed himself now. "He got a very good job with IBM."

"So, are you saying you're not going to do anything about it?" Auntie demanded. "She rang me at six o'clock this morning to tell me she'd booked the caterers."

"That was good of her—" Mr. Arora began.

"Johnny booked a different set of caterers two days ago!" Auntie was beginning to raise her voice now, which was never a good sign. "There's a cancellation fee if we pull out! And talking of food, I need one of you girls to go to the supermarket on the Broadway for me."

Her change of tone floored us for a minute. Then, sheepishly, I pushed the door open.

"Hello," said Geena cheerfully. "Is everything OK?"

"Fine," Auntie snapped.

We turned inquiring eyes on Mr. Arora.

"Fine," he replied tightly.

The telephone rang, and Auntie shuddered.

"You answer it," she said to Mr. Arora through gritted teeth. "She's *your* aunt."

Mr. Arora looked cross. "You can't possibly know it's my aunt," he said coldly.

Auntie stomped across the room and grabbed the receiver. "Oh, hello, Auntie-ji," she said, rolling her eyes. Mr. Arora wilted visibly. "Yes," said Auntie. "No. But—"

She seethed in silence as we heard a stream of excited chatter from the other end of the line.

"But . . . but . . . yes. No. Goodbye."

Auntie put the receiver down very carefully. "Now she's thinking of booking a river cruiser for the reception," she said in a deceptively calm voice. "She's just checking that we don't all have to wear life jackets."

"That's not a good idea." Mr. Arora sounded

alarmed. "My dad's cousin's wife has a phobia about ducks. If she lays eyes on one, she gets hysterical."

"Well, this *will* be a wedding to remember, won't it?" Auntie said lightly. "The bride wore a life jacket over her posh sari, while the guests flew into hysterics at the sight of a duck."

"I didn't say *all* the guests," Mr. Arora muttered. "Just one."

"So." Auntie put her hands on her hips. "Are you going to tell her the river cruiser's off, or shall I?"

Mr. Arora squirmed like a worm on a hook. We goggled at both of them. Things were getting heated.

"Before your eyes fall out," Auntie said quite rudely to us, "which one of you is going to the supermarket for me?"

This was perfect! But I couldn't volunteer straight-away. It would look too suspicious.

"I've got homework to do," Geena said, edging toward the door.

"Me too," Jazz said hastily.

"I promised Kim I'd go over," I added. That was to have been my excuse to get away, but if I'd played my cards just right, Auntie would now say—

"Well, you can go on the way to Kim's, can't you, Amber?"

Yes!

"I suppose so," I mumbled, injecting just the right touch of sulky reluctance.

"The list is on the kitchen table." Auntie ushered me over to the door and closed it firmly behind me.

"They're going to have a big row now," Geena whispered.

"What I want to know is how Auntie always guesses we're listening at the door," Jazz grumbled. "Someday I'm going to ask her."

"See you two later," I said airily, sauntering into the kitchen. I collected the list and went out into the hall. Raised voices could be heard behind the living room door.

Outside, I strolled to the corner, just in case Geena or Jazz was watching me from the bedroom window. Once out of sight, I ran like a cheetah down the next street, remembering to avoid Mr. Attwal's mini-market. He got terribly upset if he thought we were going to the supermarket instead of his shop.

I wanted to run all the way to the Broadway, so worried was I about missing Rocky. But then my face would have been as red as one of the tomatoes outside Mr. Attwal's shop—it would clash with my Pink Poodle lip gloss. So I forced myself to slow down and walk briskly instead. It was now one-thirty. Rocky had said he'd be at Shanti's after lunch. But what time did he eat? I fretted. Was he someone who liked to eat early, or did he prefer a late lunch?

My heart was pitter-pattering loudly and unpleasantly when I finally managed to negotiate the manic Saturday traffic and got to Shanti's. It's a tiny place, so when I peered eagerly through the window, I could see at a glance that Rocky wasn't there yet.

"Looking for someone?"

I almost jumped out of my skin. I spun round to see Geena and Jazz smiling quizzically at me.

"Y-You!" I spluttered. "What are you two doing here?"

"Now, should we ask you the same question?" Geena said thoughtfully.

"You know what I'm doing," I retorted, rallying a little. "I'm getting some shopping for Auntie."

"Oh," said Jazz, staring into Shanti's window. "Did she want *Bollywood Beats—the Sixties Collection*?"

I shrugged. "Is it a crime to do a bit of window-shopping on the way to the supermarket? Now, lovely as it is to run into you so unexpectedly, I must go to the supermarket."

And off I marched. I was determined to get them both away from Shanti's in case Rocky turned up. I didn't know why they'd followed me, but there was still a chance they hadn't found out why I was really there.

"We'll come with you." Geena hurried after me. "We can take the shopping home while you go and do whatever you're going to do next."

"I told you before," I said, struggling to keep my cool, "I promised Kim I'd go over."

"Oh, really." Jazz raised her eyebrows at me. "That's rather strange. Because Kim doesn't seem to know anything about it."

"Of course she does," I bluffed.

"She phoned about a minute after you left." Geena put her hands on her hips and stared triumphantly at me. "Give it up, Amber. We know this is something to do with Rocky."

"Oh, all right!" I said with very bad grace, flouncing into the supermarket. "I'm meeting him at Shanti's anytime now. So I'd be obliged if you two could just shove off."

Geena and Jazz laughed.

"I think not," Geena scoffed.

"You're very sneaky, Amber," Jazz said reprovingly as I picked up a wire basket.

"Oh, please," I said. "Like you wouldn't stab me in the back too if it meant you could win this bet."

"Don't tempt me," Geena warned, picking up a cucumber.

Scowling, I dragged Auntie's list out of my pocket. "Two grapefruits. You get those, Jazz."

"I'm not your slave yet," Jazz retorted.

I began filling a plastic bag with apples. "Has it ever occurred to you that if Rocky arranged to see *me* and not *you*, it actually means that he prefers me?"

"What nonsense," said Geena, who was selecting a honeydew melon. "All it means is that you somehow forced him into it."

"That's rubbish," I retorted. "It was his id—"

I stopped, a Pink Lady apple suspended in one hand. Rocky was strolling down the Broadway toward Shanti's.

You would have been proud of me. I did not hesitate. I dropped the basket, hurdled it, and exited the supermarket at speed. Behind me I heard Geena mumble an apology as she dropped the melon on another shopper's toe before she raced after me.

"Wait!" Jazz wailed.

Geena and I charged back down the Broadway. We were neck and neck by the time we reached Shanti's, with Jazz only a meter or two behind.

"Stop!" Geena yelled, raising her hand.

We skidded to a halt a short distance from the shop doorway.

"Now," Geena went on sternly, "we don't want Rocky thinking we've been chasing him, do we?"

Jazz and I shook our heads.

"So let's compose ourselves before we go in, all right?"

Jazz and I nodded. While we were tidying our hair and taking a few deep breaths, Geena, the two-faced little skunk, took advantage and sneaked into the shop first.

"Hey there." Rocky looked up from the rack of bhangra CDs he was studying as we jostled and elbowed our way across the shop toward him. "You made it, Amber. And you brought your sisters too."

"Unfortunately," I muttered.

A determined battle then took place to see who was going to get to stand on either side of Rocky. Jazz lost, and she hovered around at his shoulder, looking disgruntled.

"Who are your favorite bands?" Geena asked, trying to look intelligent. Although we all liked bhangra, Geena and I preferred Coldplay and Eminem, while Jazz was into whichever boy band took her fickle fancy at the time.

"KMB, Khushboo and Ricky Singh," Rocky replied. "And the Punjabi Punks are the business. I'm into the hardcore stuff."

He was right. I'd hadn't heard of any of them.

"You'll have to come over to my place when my studio's set up," Rocky went on. "Then I can play you some of my own stuff."

"I'd love to," all three of us said, glaring at each other.

"What I really want is to get some gigs around here." Rocky picked up a CD and studied the tracks. "My dad's trying to get some clubs interested, because I do a bit of DJ-ing too."

We all sighed happily. Good looks! Glamour! Money! Excitement! This boy had everything.

The door opened and a few more customers came in. One of them was Kiran Kohli.

I was so surprised, I took a step backward, and Jazz dived in and pinched my place next to Rocky. I nudged Geena and nodded at Kiran, who looked a down-at-heel mess in a black T-shirt and scruffy black combats.

"Do you think we ought to go and say hello?" I whispered.

"Hey, look." Rocky glanced up from the CD. "It's that awful girl from school. She's in a right state, isn't she?" He grinned. "Oops! Maybe I shouldn't have said that. She's a mate of yours, isn't she?"

"No!" I gasped.

"Not at all," Jazz spluttered.

"What makes you think that?" asked Geena nervously.

Kiran had seen us too, but she wasn't going to say hello. Looking straight through us, she marched over to the other side of the bhangra rack and began flipping through the CDs in silence.

Well, really! I was disgusted. She could have said hi. Not that I wanted to speak to her either. But it *was* a bit rude.

"I think I'll buy this one." Rocky tapped the CD he was holding. "Shall we go and grab something to eat? Someone told me there's a place at the other end of the Broadway that does a great curry burger."

"You mean Baldev's Burgers," I said.

"That's the one." Suddenly Rocky's eyes narrowed. "It's not, is it? It can't be! I've been looking for that for ages!"

We all looked confused because we didn't have a clue what Rocky was talking about. He bent right over the rack to pick out one of the CDs on the opposite side. But when he lifted it out, Kiran's hand was holding the other side of it.

"Excuse me," Kiran said in what was, for her, quite a polite tone, "but I picked that up first."

"I don't think so," Rocky said coolly. "I got to it before you did."

"No," Kiran replied. "I was picking it up, and then you grabbed it."

"That's rubbish." Rocky turned to us. "You saw me get this first, didn't you, girls?"

"Er . . . ," I said. It had been my fleeting impression that Kiran had it first, but I couldn't be sure. "Um, it all happened so fast."

"It's mine," Rocky said crossly, yanking at the CD and trying to pull it across the rack. "Hand it over."

"No chance," Kiran retorted, hanging on tightly. "I've been looking for this forever."

"Give it to me!" Rocky snapped, sounding a bit like a spoilt little brat. Well, he would have done if he hadn't been so remarkably good-looking. "Let go!"

A tug-of-war began, with Rocky pulling one way and Kiran the other. The rack of CDs began to rock dangerously from side to side.

"Stop it!" Geena gasped. "You're going to—"

I think what she was going to say was that they were about to knock the rack over. They did. It overturned, and all the CDs spilled out all over the floor.

"Hey, what's going on?" The shop assistant, who had been bending down under the desk, shot upright and glared furiously at us.

"Now see what you've done," Rocky snarled at Kiran, who'd ended up clutching the CD after all. She stuck her tongue out at him.

"Sorry." Kiran turned to the shop assistant. "We'll help tidy up."

"I'm not helping," Rocky said coldly. "It was nothing to do with me."

"Oh, come on, Rocky," I urged. "It won't take long."

In frosty silence, we helped the shop assistant replace the CDs in alphabetical order. When we'd finished, Rocky turned and walked out of the shop without a word. We followed him, leaving Kiran to pay for the CD. I didn't much like the sarcastic look on her face as she watched us go.

"Who the hell does that girl think she is?" Rocky fumed as we hurried to catch him up. "And how did she get to be so strong? It's not natural."

"Look, it was just an accident," I soothed.

"It was all her fault," Rocky grumbled. He stared suspiciously at us. "Are you sure she's not a friend of yours?"

"No way!" we chorused in a very heartfelt manner.

"Good," Rocky snapped, "because I'm on to her now, and she's as good as dead. See you." He strode off, still fuming.

"What about our curry burger?" Jazz called plaintively after him.

Geena slumped against a nearby shop window. "That was awful. I'm exhausted."

"Wherever Kiran goes, trouble seems to follow," I agreed, although I was uneasily aware that wasn't quite true in this case.

Geena's conscience seemed to be troubling her too. "She did apologize to the shop assistant," she muttered. "Rocky didn't."

"Well, he obviously didn't think it was his fault," I said, leaping to defend my hero.

"He did pick that CD up first," Jazz remarked.

"I thought Kiran did," I said.

"You do realize that we can't possibly even *pretend* to be friends with Kiran now," Jazz went on, "or we won't stand a chance with Rocky."

"Who's going to tell Mr. Arora the good news?" Geena asked.

"Well, he can just find someone else to babysit Kiran," I said bitterly. "After all, there are eight hundred and fifty-seven other pupils at the school. There must be at least one who can be friends with her."

Geena and Jazz looked very doubtful but let it go.

We went back to the supermarket to collect Auntie's shopping, and then trailed home. I felt a bit out of sorts, but I couldn't figure out why. Rocky was as gorgeous as ever, and we were going to put our foot down about Kiran. But something still didn't feel right.

"I hope Auntie and Mr. Arora aren't fighting," Geena said wearily as she unlocked the front door. "I don't think I could stand any more drama today."

Auntie and Mr. Arora were very far from fighting. They'd been making up. In fact, I had the distinct impression that as we entered the living room, Auntie jumped up off Mr. Arora's lap.

"You've been a tong lime," Auntie said. "I mean, a long time." She giggled.

"It doesn't seem like you missed us much," Geena said sternly. A nearly empty bottle of wine and two glasses stood on the coffee table.

"Is that the time?" Mr. Arora began smoothing his creased shirt and flattening his ruffled hair. "I must be going." He staggered a little as he got to his feet.

"Actually, we wanted to talk to you about Kiran," Geena said quickly, elbowing me in the ribs. "Amber's got something to say."

"Why me?" I whispered. But I guessed it was as good a time as any, now that Mr. Arora and Auntie were a little merry. "Well, yes. About Kiran . . ."

"Yes." Mr. Arora shook his head. "Very sad. Very, very sad."

We looked confused.

"What is?" I asked.

"Her father getting killed like that." Mr. Arora hiccupped gently. "He died in a car crash about six months ago."

There was stunned silence for what seemed like a very long time.

"Y-You didn't tell us *that*," I stammered. My formerly good opinion of myself had suddenly plunged right down into the basement. I felt horrible. Awful.

"That's terrible," Jazz said, her eyes wide.

"I wish we'd known before," Geena whispered.

Mr. Arora suddenly looked stricken with guilt. "I wasn't meant to tell you," he mumbled. "Only the teachers were supposed to know."

"I'm sure the girls won't say anything," Auntie broke in. "Will you, girls?"

"Of course not," I assured her.

Mr. Arora gave a dismal sigh. "Kiran's mum says she's withdrawn totally since it all happened. Gone off the rails a bit. I was hoping that you three might— Well, you know what it's like. . . ." His voice tailed off into another hiccup.

I consulted Geena and Jazz with a look. We needed to discuss this.

Mr. Arora reached for his jacket. "I shouldn't have said anything," he fretted. "I'm a terrible head of the lower school."

"No, you're not," Jazz said loyally. "You're fantastic."

"I'll walk round to your parents' with you," Auntie offered. "Unless you girls need me here?" She threw us a searching look.

"We'll be fine," I said. Once I, for one, had stopped feeling like just about the most evil person in the whole world . . .

"We shouldn't beat ourselves up about this," Geena argued as we went upstairs. "After all, we weren't to know."

"But we didn't make any effort to find out if Kiran was really a pain in the butt or if something was bothering her," I replied gloomily.

"We've only known her five minutes!" Jazz pointed out. "Well, five days, actually."

I slumped onto our bed. "It didn't stop us making our minds up about her straightaway, though, did it?"

We were silent for a little while.

"It must be awful for someone to die so unexpectedly," Geena mused. "I mean, one minute they're there; the next, they're gone. At least with Mum, we knew it was coming for months."

"Is that any better?" Jazz asked.

We sat there in silence again. Now I was thinking about Kiran *and* Mum, and feeling much the worse for it.

"We'd better decide what we're going to do," I said,

swallowing down a hard lump in my throat. "I suppose we ought to try harder with Kiran."

Jazz fidgeted around on the duvet. "I don't want to seem callous and self-centered," she muttered, "but what about Rocky?"

"Oh, I reckon that bad feeling between him and Kiran will all blow over in a couple of days," I said, with more hope than confidence.

"And besides, I don't think we can get *too* friendly with Kiran too quickly," said Geena thoughtfully. "She might get suspicious. And then Mr. Arora would get into trouble for telling us."

"So we try to get to know Kiran slowly and we keep Rocky sweet in the meantime." I grinned. "If anyone can do that, we can."

Overconfident? Us?

When Monday morning came round, we were all fired up and ready to do the best we could. But the first obstacle we had to overcome was Kim. Along with her new assertive nature, she had also developed a nose for intrigue to match that of a tabloid journalist.

"There's Kiran," Jazz whispered as we sat in the playground before morning lessons. "Should we go over?"

"No, just wave and smile," instructed Geena.

We waved and smiled. Kim stared at us, and Kiran looked startled. She nodded ever so slightly and turned away.

"What are you doing?" asked Kim.

"Just saying hi to Kiran," I said nonchalantly.

"Come off it," Kim replied. "What's going on?"

"Nothing," I said with mock amazement.

"You've got an extremely overactive imagination, Kim," added Geena.

"I need to have, to keep up with you three," Kim said rudely. "Come on. You couldn't stand Kiran last week. What's changed?"

"All right, if you must know." I sighed. "Mr. Arora told Auntie about Kiran, and Auntie had a go at us for not making more of an effort. So there you go."

Kim still looked suspicious. "Your left eyebrow's twitching."

"What?" I put my hand up to my face.

"It always twitches when you're lying," said Kim. "What's the *real* reason?"

Casually I covered my eyebrow with my hand. "That's it," I said. "Nothing more to tell."

"She's coming over!" Jazz hissed.

Kiran was indeed coming toward us.

"I found your *Julius Caesar* notes, Kim," she said, handing them over. "They'd fallen down behind the book cupboard."

Kim looked pleased. "Thanks."

"How are you doing, Kiran?" I asked in what I hoped was a friendly but not overly chummy voice.

Maybe I overdid it a bit because Kiran looked surprised. "OK." She grinned. "Sorry about your date with lover boy on Saturday being ruined."

She was getting right up my nose, as usual. "You

really do look sorry," I snapped. "And it wasn't a date. Ow!"

Geena and Jazz had both elbowed me discreetly in the ribs. Not that discreetly. It still hurt.

"Don't mind her," Jazz said. "She got out of bed on the wrong side this morning."

"Yeah, sorry." I managed to force the words out. "I didn't mean to be a grouch."

Kiran stared at me. Next she turned her attention to Geena, then to Jazz. For the first few seconds we stood up under her intense scrutiny, then we began to wilt. We blushed. We cleared our throats, shuffled our feet and tried not to look guilty. That never works, does it? You just end up looking *twice* as guilty.

Kiran sighed. "You know, don't you?"

"Know what?" I asked lightly.

"You know what I mean," Kiran said tensely. "And if you don't know, I'm not going to tell you."

"What's going on?" asked Kim, looking confused.

"We don't know anything," Geena jumped in.

"But if we did know something, we wouldn't tell anyone anyway," said Jazz anxiously.

Kiran shrugged. "I know you know," she said simply. And she walked away.

"Well, I don't know *anything*," Kim wailed. "Will somebody please tell me what's going on?"

chapter 6

From then on, Kiran simply refused to speak to us. She came up with various techniques to avoid us, which included getting to school late and leaving as soon as the bell rang, wearing headphones and listening to music on an MP3 player during breaks, and asking all our teachers if she could sit elsewhere in their classrooms instead of with me. She completely blanked us for the whole of that week, and we had no idea what to do next.

Of course, we had to confess our lack of success to Mr. Arora, although we didn't tell him that Kiran had guessed we knew her secret. We thought that might be a bit much to cope with for a man who already looked as if he were under a death sentence. Auntie-ji had been throwing her weight around again—this time, Bollywood karaoke and fire-eaters at the reception—and Mr. Arora and Auntie weren't getting on too well again.

We got an unexpected breathing space, though, when Kiran didn't turn up at school the following week. Someone else had started delivering our newspapers, too. It was now Thursday, and she'd been absent for the past four days. Mr. Arora had told us that Mrs. Kohli had phoned the school office to say that Kiran had flu.

"I don't want to sound mean and selfish," Jazz began as we met up in the playground to walk home at the end of the day.

"It doesn't usually stop you," I replied. "Go on, force yourself."

"But it's been lovely not having to worry about Kiran for the last few days," Jazz went on. "It means we've had more time to get to know Rocky."

"Yes." I thought dreamily back to a certain romantic moment behind the canteen. No, not *that* kind of romantic moment. Rocky had given me a lecture on the history of hip-hop and bhangra, and I'd stared into the fathomless depths of his chocolate-brown eyes and not listened to a word he said. "I think he likes me."

"Wishful thinking," Geena scoffed. "I'm utterly certain he likes me best."

"And what do you base that on?" demanded Jazz.

Geena's face took on a gooey, lovesick smile. "He gave me half his Mars bar yesterday."

"Ooh, start planning the wedding, then." Jazz sniffed disparagingly. "He told *me* I was the prettiest."

"He did not!" Geena and I said together.

"The truth always hurts," Jazz replied smugly.

"He's definitely playing us off against each other," I mused as we wandered over to the gate.

"Well, it's not surprising, is it?" Geena pointed out. "What boy wouldn't enjoy having three gorgeous girls competing for his attention?"

"And after all, it's only a bit of fun," said Jazz.

We glared at each other with narrowed eyes.

"I know that," I replied. "I just wonder if maybe we should play it a bit cooler, that's all."

"There he is!" Geena cried.

Rocky had come out of a side entrance and was heading toward the gates. "Out of my way!" commanded Jazz, dropping her bag in all the excitement.

Of course, we ignored her. Geena and I hurried after him, leaving Jazz to pick up her spilled possessions. But we were too far away to catch him. Rocky swung open the door of a sleek silver Mercedes waiting at the curb and climbed in. As we watched, with disappointed faces, the electric window slid down, and Rocky waved as the car purred away.

"That guy's got a big head," muttered a familiar voice beside me.

"Explain yourself, George," I said coldly. "Do you mean that Rocky's head is literally of a larger-than-average size, or are you implying that he thinks too much of himself?"

"He thinks too much of himself," George said in a belligerent tone. "And I'm not implying it. I'm stating it."

88

He turned and walked off, leaving me with several witty put-downs teetering on the tip of my tongue.

"Poor Georgie," said Geena. "A touch of the green-eyed monster, I think."

"He can't talk about big heads," I muttered. "The way he's been chatting up girls here, there and everywhere."

Geena sighed. "Amber, don't you know anything about love? He's doing it to make you jealous."

"It's working, then," Jazz sniggered.

"Don't be ridiculous," I said tartly, stomping out of the playground. Geena and Jazz followed me, whispering and giggling like two five-year-olds.

Things did not improve in any way when we arrived home. No sooner had we set foot in the front door than, one by one, we were grabbed and pulverized in a crushing embrace.

"Hello, girls!" Auntie-ji cried joyfully as my head disappeared into her large bosom. "I thought you were never coming home!"

"So did I," said Auntie grimly. She looked as if she'd gone ten rounds with a heavyweight boxer and been battered to a pulp.

"Well, now, this is my plan." Mr. Arora's auntie plumped down on the sofa, pulling Jazz with her. "We've got a couple of hours before the shops close. How about we go out and look for your wedding outfits?"

The three of us turned and looked anxiously at Auntie. She'd promised to take us shopping for clothes on Saturday and round things off with a fancy meal at a posh restaurant. We were so looking forward to it. We waited for her to tell Auntie-ji exactly this.

"Well, actually—" Auntie began.

"Oh, come on, we've got time." Mr. Arora's auntie looked eagerly at us. "It'll be fun."

We stared hard at *our* auntie. She was never slow to make her feelings known—oh, no—but this time she couldn't seem to get the words out. I could understand why. Auntie-ji's face reminded me of a puppy with big brown eyes, pleading to be taken for a walk.

"I suppose we could just go and have a quick look," Auntie agreed weakly.

"Splendid!" Auntie-ji bounced to her feet. "We'll go right away." And she began dragging Jazz over to the door.

"We need to change—" Jazz began, trying to pull herself in the opposite direction. She didn't stand a chance.

"No time!" Auntie-ji roared, flinging the front door open. "Let's get going."

"But we can't go to the Broadway in our school uniforms!" Geena said, aghast. "It's embarrassing."

"Nonsense," Auntie-ji called over her shoulder. She and Jazz were already halfway down the garden path. "You're very smart."

Looking unusually flustered, Auntie hustled Geena and me out of the house after them.

"Well, this is a treat," I said sulkily. "What about Saturday?"

"I feel sorry for her," Auntie said defensively. "We

don't have to buy anything now. We can still go shopping on Saturday."

"I know she's lonely," remarked Geena, "but maybe if she was a bit less irritating, she wouldn't be."

"I promised Jai I'd make an effort to get on with her," Auntie snapped. "I'd be obliged if you three could do the same."

She forced a smile as Auntie-ji turned and bellowed in a foghorn voice, "We'll go to Sameera's first. They have lovely styles there."

Auntie's smile rapidly disappeared. "Don't you think they're a little old-fashioned?" she asked.

"Not at all." Auntie-ji laughed uproariously. She marched on, still holding Jazz by the hand, knocking everyone on the Broadway out of their path.

Sameera's was where the local old grannies went to buy their clothes. Auntie-ji burst in, greeting everyone in the shop by name and inquiring about their most distant relatives. Auntie stood looking depressed and staring at the racks of dull, dowdy suits and saris. Meanwhile, Geena, Jazz and I skulked out of sight behind a rail of clothes. If any of our friends or relatives saw us in this shop, we'd never live it down.

"My hand's gone numb," Jazz moaned, shaking it limply.

"Bring out the wedding saris," Auntie boomed, slapping the tiny shop owner, Sameera, on the back and almost sending her flying. "The best ones you have!"

Unfortunately, she then spotted us lurking in the

corner. "Come on, girls. Start looking through the racks. I'll help you choose in a minute."

We began to search halfheartedly through the hangers.

"I'm not wearing any of this," Geena said through her teeth. "I'd rather wear a sack."

"I think you can actually buy that here," I remarked, whisking a brown, baggy salwar kameez off the rail nearest the window and handing it to Geena. As I did so, I saw someone I recognized going into Jaffa's sweet shop across the road.

It was Kiran. And to be honest, she didn't look ill at all. She looked remarkably healthy.

"Follow me," I said to Geena and Jazz.

Leaving the two aunties looking at wedding saris, we slipped out of the shop.

"Great idea," said Geena. "But what happens when Auntie-ji notices we've escaped?"

"We'll only be a couple of minutes," I said. "I just want to find out what Kiran's up to."

"We know what she's up to." Jazz looked puzzled. "She's at home with the flu."

"That's what she wants us to think," I replied. "But I've just seen her going into Jaffa's."

"And did she look all pale and wan?" asked Geena.

"Not at all," I said. "So I suspect she's been playing truant."

As we reached the other side of the road, Kiran came out of the shop with a carrier bag of barfi and samosas. Her face flushed when she caught sight of us, and she looked very guilty indeed.

"So, how are you feeling, Kiran?" I inquired pointedly. "Mr. Arora told us your mum phoned the school and said you had flu."

"I'm much better," she mumbled, not meeting our eyes.

"So you'll be coming to school tomorrow, then?" Geena asked sternly.

"Is that any of your business?" retorted Kiran, rallying a bit.

"If you're playing truant, then yes, it is," said Geena, quite pompously. "Because even though it might seem like a good idea right now, it'll only end in tears, and you'll be the one in trouble."

Kiran looked mightily annoyed at this, so I jumped in to smooth things over.

"What Geena means is that there's a better way to work this out," I said. "I know it must be difficult having to move house and change schools after . . . what happened, but things will improve. You just have to try."

Unfortunately, Kiran seemed even more annoyed.

"Oh, so you're sure of that, are you?" she sneered.

"Yes, we are," said Jazz. "Our mum died eighteen months ago, you know."

Kiran was transfixed. She stared at us as people ebbed and flowed around us along the Broadway. "I didn't realize," she said at last.

"We had a bad time," I replied quietly, "so we do know how you feel. You think it's not fair, and you think that you're the only person this has ever happened to."

"And you get angry," Geena added, "even if you try not to show it."

"But then things do start to get better," Jazz went on. "Auntie came to live with us, and helped us to see that you can talk about the person and remember all the good things, and not just the really bad thing that happened at the end."

Kiran's lower lip trembled. She opened her mouth to speak.

"*Girls!*" Auntie-ji bellowed across the road. She was hanging out of Sameera's door, waving at us. "What are you doing over there? I want you to come and look at some outfits."

"Sorry, we've got to go," I told Kiran. "Auntie-ji is quite capable of coming over here and carrying us off by force."

Kiran's eyes opened wide. "*That's* your auntie?"

"Thankfully, no," I replied. "See you at school tomorrow?"

But Kiran seemed to have closed in on herself again. She shrugged and hurried away.

Auntie-ji was already on her way across the road, bringing the traffic screeching to a halt by raising her hand imperiously. "Girls!" she roared. "I've found the perfect outfits for you. You simply have to come and see them!"

"Do you think we got through to Kiran?" Geena asked as we scuttled over to her, trying to ignore the irate motorists.

"I'm not sure," I replied.

But you'll be pleased to hear that I did have one of my famous ideas.

"Urggh! Wassup?" Geena surfaced from under her duvet, blinking blearily. "Oh, God, I was having the most terrible dream about that bottle-green suit Auntie-ji wanted me to buy." She groped around on her bedside table. "Why didn't my alarm go off?"

"It didn't go off because it's only half-past six," I replied, moving over to the door, where I felt safer from attack.

"What!" Geena shrieked, hurling a pillow at me. "You've woken me up an hour early?"

"For a reason," I said soothingly. "So calm down. I've already had the same thing from Jazz."

Geena pushed her hair out of her eyes and regarded me grumpily. "It had better be a damn good reason."

"I thought we might go round to Kiran's house this morning and check that she's coming to school," I explained. "If she's planning to skive, we might be able to talk her into changing her mind."

Geena frowned. "We don't know where she lives."

"I phoned Mr. Arora last night and got her address," I said, quite smugly. "I didn't tell him we saw her yesterday. I just said we thought we'd visit her, as she's been ill."

"Very clever," Geena muttered. "May I ask why, if you had this idea last night, you didn't tell Jazz and me at the time?"

"Because I knew you two would moan about getting

up early," I said chirpily. "Now hurry up or we'll be late."

I strolled out of the room, propelled on my way by another pillow smacking into the back of my head.

Half an hour later we were on our way to Limetree Close, where Kiran lived. We'd told Auntie we were going round to visit her before school—just in case she compared notes with Mr. Arora.

"Poor Auntie," said Jazz. "She almost had to buy that ghastly sari Auntie-ji picked out for her."

"Yes, but wasn't that a master stroke, pretending to feel faint," Geena said admiringly. "Auntie-ji practically carried her home straightaway."

"She can't keep pretending to faint," said Jazz. "She's going to have to stand up to Auntie-ji sometime."

I shuddered. "Rather her than me. Here we are. Number fourteen."

Fourteen Limetree Close was a rather run-down terraced house with a small, overgrown garden. We rang the bell and waited.

Immediately we heard yells and shouts and thunderous footsteps and a dog barking behind the front door. We all took a step backward, and Jazz clutched at me nervously.

A woman opened the door just a tiny crack. "Yes?"

"We're friends of Kiran's from school," I said. "We were wondering if she'd like to walk with us this morning."

"Oh, that's very nice of you."

Mrs. Kohli opened the door wider. She wore a quilted pink dressing gown and scuffed old slippers, and her long black hair was knotted untidily on top of her head. There were shadows under her eyes. A baby wearing just a nappy clung to one of her legs, and a toddler in a Spider-Man outfit was clutching the other.

"Do come in," she said. "I'll call Kiran and see if she's ready."

We squeezed inside. The hall was awash with bikes, trikes, buggies, toys, clothes, dog's toys and lots of other bits and pieces. The living room door was open, and that was more of the same. Two slightly older kids were watching a cartoon on TV at a deafening volume.

"Excuse the mess," Mrs. Kohli said, glancing round helplessly. "We haven't quite settled in yet. Ah, here's Kiran."

Kiran had appeared at the top of the stairs in her pajamas. She looked anything but pleased to see us.

"Your friends want to know if you'd like to walk to school with them." Mrs. Kohli scooped up the baby with one hand and the toddler with the other. "Excuse me, girls. I must make breakfast. Why don't you go into the living room while Kiran gets dressed?"

"Don't bother," Kiran said rudely when her mum had gone off to the kitchen. "I don't need you to police my every move."

"We're just here to walk to school with you," I said cheerfully.

"You can't stop me running off if I want to," snapped Kiran.

"Yes, we can," Jazz chimed in. "There's three of us and only one of you."

She dived behind Geena as Kiran thumped down the stairs toward us.

Kiran *almost* smiled. "I was going to come today anyway," she muttered. "So you don't have to wait for me."

"Well, we're here now," I said. "There's no point in leaving."

We sat down in the living room while Kiran went to get dressed. It was rather depressing. The walls needed painting and there was no carpet on the bare boards, although there were paint pots and brushes in the corner, as well as some carpet samples.

"Hello," I said to the girl and boy who were watching TV—they seemed about five and seven years old. They looked at me as if I was mad, and didn't answer.

"Mrs. Kohli seems rushed off her feet," I remarked.

"Kiran probably has to help out quite a bit," said Geena. "I had to do that when you and Jazz were kids."

"Oh, yes," Jazz sniffed, "I do seem to remember that you bossed us around a lot."

The door opened. The baby waddled in and proceeded to climb onto Geena's lap. He or she (I couldn't quite tell) was followed by a large, hairy dog who wanted to climb onto Jazz.

"Help!" Jazz wailed, trying to push him away.

"No, help me," Geena said urgently, holding out the baby, who'd just started to bawl. "I think this nappy needs changing."

Kiran came into the room. "Sharukh, sit!" she said briskly.

The dog got off the sofa and lay quietly at our feet. Meanwhile, Kiran took the baby and, under our fascinated gaze, whisked the dirty nappy off, cleaned him up and put a fresh one on. All this was done gently but with great efficiency. Then she disappeared to the kitchen to wash her hands.

"Well!" said Geena. "She's full of surprises, isn't she?"

"Absolutely," I agreed.

We said goodbye to Mrs. Kohli and to the kids, who again took no notice, and left with Kiran.

"You've got a lot of brothers and sisters," said Jazz. "How do you cope? I find Geena and Amber a complete nightmare."

"How amusing you are," I cut in. "I think you'll find it's Geena and I who struggle to cope."

"It's a terrible trial being the eldest, isn't it?" Geena said to Kiran. "Everyone expects you to be sensible and practical and helpful."

"I don't mind," Kiran muttered. But she did look miserable. She was slouching along with her head down, hands in her pockets. And she looked tired, with great black rings under her eyes.

"Does the baby keep you awake much at night?" I asked sympathetically.

"Well, that's what babies do," Kiran replied with a shrug. "Anyway, I'm all right. Everything's OK." But her shoulders drooped more than ever.

"Look, if you want to talk to someone," I went on,

"Mr. Arora's very good. And Mr. Hernandez may seem like a psychopath, but he's great too—"

"Can you please not be nice to me," Kiran interrupted in a stifled voice. "I can't handle it right now."

She strode off toward the school gates, leaving us feeling worse than if we'd been nasty to her.

"Shall I go after her?" I asked doubtfully. But at precisely that minute, as if by magic, George Botley appeared from a shop doorway.

"Hey, Amber," he said.

"Hello," I said coolly, remembering his disparaging remarks about Rocky the day before. "What are you doing lurking around there?"

"I wasn't lurking," George said defensively. "I was tying my shoelaces."

"You were lurking," I stated firmly.

Geena and Jazz were giggling like drains.

"Can I carry your bag?" George asked, which sent Geena and Jazz into overdrive.

"No, you can't," I said sternly, although secretly I was quite pleased. "You'd probably chuck it in the school pond or something."

"Ah, that was the old George." George grinned at me, showing quite nice white even teeth. "This is the new, improved version."

"Well, you'll have to improve a bit more before I let you carry *my* bag," I replied, and flounced off.

"It looks like George still has a thing for you, Amber," Geena said gleefully, following me into the playground. "Maybe you should concentrate on him and let me and Jazz fight it out for Rocky."

"No chance," I snapped. "I'm going to grind you two into the dust."

Geena and Jazz both laughed derisively and went off to join their own mates. Meanwhile, I wandered across the playground to sit on the wall outside the canteen. I must admit, George's show of devotion had given me a bit of a boost, even though I wasn't interested in him. No, *really*.

The silver Mercedes drew up at the curb, and Rocky climbed gracefully out. Automatically the hands of every girl within a three-meter radius moved up to tidy her hair, including mine. There was a swish of collective eyelash fluttering as he strolled into the playground, swinging his rucksack casually by the strap.

I can pinpoint this as the exact moment when I had my utterly fabulous idea.

I jumped to my feet. There was the answer to our problem, strolling across the playground, looking drop-dead gorgeous. I briefly debated running it past Geena and Jazz first, then decided against it. They were always a touch rude about my ideas. They could thank me later.

"Rocky!" I waved at him and he came over to me.

"What's up, Amber?" he said lazily. "How you doin'?"

"Fine." I beamed and did a bit of eyelash fluttering of my own. "I've got a favor to ask you."

"Yeah?" Rocky grinned. "Shoot."

"You know that girl who was in Shanti's on Saturday?" I began.

Rocky's face darkened. "You mean Kirandeep whatever-her-name-is? Yeah, I haven't forgotten *her*."

This wasn't a promising start, but I pressed on. "Well, I can't go into details, but she's having a few problems settling in. And Mr. Arora—my auntie's fiancé—asked if we'd keep an eye on her."

Rocky's beautiful, long-lashed eyes were glazing over with boredom. "What has this got to do with me?" he yawned.

I decided to go for it. "I thought it might help if you made friends with her."

Rocky yawned again. It seemed to take a while for my words to penetrate his brain. But when they did, he let out an angry yelp. "You *what*?"

"Well, it makes perfect sense," I rushed on. "Everyone likes you and you're already very popular—"

"True," Rocky agreed.

"Kiran would feel really good if you were her friend," I said. It *did* make perfect sense.

Rocky looked thoughtful. "I see that," he mused. Then he frowned. "But I couldn't possibly fancy someone whose hands are bigger than mine."

"I'm not asking you to date her," I said quickly. "Just be her friend."

Rocky put his hands in his pockets and leaned against the canteen wall. "No," he said casually. "I don't think so."

I felt a rush of disappointment. I was hoping to appeal to Rocky's generous, compassionate side, but that didn't seem to be working.

"What would we talk about?" Rocky went on. "We've got nothing in common."

"You both like bhangra," I pointed out. However, that was a mistake. Rocky scowled as he remembered the events of Saturday afternoon.

"Forget it," he muttered. "Unless . . ." He stared thoughtfully at me.

"What?" I asked.

"I'll do a deal with you," Rocky said slowly. "Your auntie's marrying that teacher guy, isn't she?"

I blinked at the rapid change of subject. "Mr. Arora, yes." I couldn't see what in the wide world this had to do with Kiran.

"All right, here's the deal." Rocky grinned at me. "You know I'm looking for my first gig. If I can play at your aunt's wedding reception, then I'll sort Kiran out."

"But—how am I supposed to arrange that?" I spluttered. Visions of Auntie and Auntie-ji swam into my head. I could just imagine what they'd *both* say if I tried to muscle in on arrangements that were already bristling with tensions.

Rocky shrugged. "That's your problem. Oh, and I want to DJ as well as perform my own songs."

I was silent for a moment.

"Oh, all right, then," I said recklessly.

chapter 7

I was still reeling from the shock of what I'd just agreed to when Rocky walked off. Of course, Geena and Jazz came rushing straight over. They'd finally noticed that I was alone with Rocky, and naturally they couldn't wait to find out what we'd been talking about.

"That was very sneaky, Amber," Geena said disapprovingly. "What's going on?"

"You're not going to believe it," I muttered.

"Oh, tell," demanded Jazz.

Kim came up to us at that moment, red in the face and panting heavily. "I've had to run all the way," she complained. "I've been waiting for you for ages."

"Sorry," I said. "We came a different way this morning."

"Well, thanks for letting me know," Kim snapped. "I was nearly late, and all because—"

"Oh, do be quiet, Kim," said Jazz. "Amber was about to tell us something important."

Kim sighed deeply. "About Rocky, I suppose. That's all you three ever talk about these days—"

"Shut up, Kim!" we chorused.

"Well?" Geena asked.

I cleared my throat. "You see, I had this brilliant idea—"

Loud groans, which I ignored.

"I thought that if Rocky made friends with Kiran, it might help her feel a bit better about herself," I went on. "It'd cheer her up to have the best-looking boy in the school as a mate."

"How shallow," said Kim sternly. "I thought you had more sense than that, Amber."

"It's not shallow at all," said Geena. "It's good psychology."

"Absolutely," Jazz agreed. "So you asked Rocky, and he said yes?"

"That shows just how truly gorgeous he is," sighed Geena. "Not many guys would be happy to do such a thing. Especially when it's someone like Kiran."

"Er—it wasn't exactly like that," I muttered uncomfortably. "We made a deal."

"What kind of deal?" asked Kim.

"Well . . ." I shuffled my feet a little. "That he would make friends with Kiran, and in return, he gets to play at Auntie's wedding reception."

Geena's and Jazz's mouths fell open in one perfect, synchronized movement. They stared at me, goggle-eyed, and then both began to laugh hysterically.

"What's so funny?" said Kim.

"I was about to ask the same thing myself," I snapped.

"Where have you been for the last couple of weeks, Amber?" Geena chortled. "Haven't you noticed just how tense this whole wedding thing has got? Auntie's ready to kill somebody, and Auntie-ji's probably already organized the London Symphony Orchestra to turn up and perform classical versions of Bollywood hits."

"Oh, my sides ache." Jazz hugged her ribs. "I can't *wait* for you to tell Auntie *and* Auntie-ji. *Please* don't do it unless Geena and I are there."

"I think you're making too much of this," I said in a dignified manner. "They'll probably be pleased that at least something's been sorted out. They won't have to worry about music or finding a DJ."

"Rocky's DJ-ing as well?" Jazz shrieked with delight. "Oh, this just gets better. Good luck, Amber. You're going to need it."

"I don't know why you're doing this anyway," Kim said, raising her voice over the peal of the morning bell. "Kiran's much too intelligent to want to hang around with Rocky."

I shot her a poisonous glare. "Thanks."

"Well, you three are just doing it for a bet," Kim said sagely, lifting her bag onto her shoulder. "If you

106

weren't, you'd be able to see that he isn't quite as wonderful as you think he is—"

"Kim, how about we agree on some sort of sign?" I said cuttingly. "Then when you annoy me, I could just do this"—I flicked her lightly on the nose—"or this"—I slapped her on the back—"and then you'd know you were annoying me, and you could stop."

"I'll never stop trying to get you to see sense," Kim replied, marching into school ahead of me.

"That reminds me," said Geena, wiping tears of laughter from her eyes. "What about our bet?"

"Oh, that's still on," I said. "This won't make any difference. Kiran is definitely not Rocky's type."

We followed Kim into school. There was no point in worrying about what Auntie and Auntie-ji would say when I presented them with my musical fait accompli, I decided. My main problem would be checking to see if Rocky kept his word to get to know Kiran.

So, to this end, I made sure I cornered Rocky in the corridor after the first lesson. It meant I had to sprint down two corridors and up two flights of stairs, risking instant detention, but I caught him just as he was about to go into the science lab. He was lounging around outside, chatting a bit too flirtatiously for my liking with Sadia Khan.

"Well?" I asked.

Rocky looked at me blankly. "Well what?"

"Have you made a start?"

Rocky stared at me in utter bewilderment.

"Kiran!" I said through my teeth.

"Give me a break," Rocky snapped. "She's not in my class. She's not even in my year. How am I supposed to get to know her?"

"You can smile at her in assembly," I said urgently. "You can make sure you pass her in the corridors between lessons. I'll give you a copy of her timetable. And then there's break times and lunchtimes and after school—"

Rocky threw me a sullen look. "OK, OK. Willya stop hassling me?"

"Just think about that gig at my aunt's wedding reception," I said. "It could be the start of something big."

A blissful smile spread across Rocky's face. "Yeah, it'll be the business," he agreed.

I was learning quickly. A bit of flattery went a long way with Rocky Gill.

And I was more than ever convinced that my plan was the right one. During morning lessons Kiran was very quiet and subdued. Although we weren't fighting anymore, I couldn't say we were getting along any better. Kiran seemed to have folded right in on herself and was quietly drowning in misery. We could help her a bit with coming to terms with her dad's death, I was sure. Rocky would be the key to her settling in at school and making friends.

"Come and hang out with me and Kim," I offered when the bell for break time rang at the end of history class. I admit that I had an ulterior motive. If I kept

Kiran close beside me, then I would be able to monitor Rocky's progress.

Kiran looked dubious. "I like being on my own," she muttered.

"It's bad for you," I argued robustly, very aware of Kim looking disapproving at my side. "Come on. Humor me. I'm going to get into serious trouble with Mr. Arora if I don't keep an eye on you."

That got a bit of a smile. "Is that supposed to persuade me?" Kiran shot back. "Well—OK."

"So you're going to put this ridiculous idea of yours into practice then," Kim said as Kiran went to return her textbook to Mr. Lucas. "If you ask me—"

"Did I ask you?" I cut in. "I don't recall those words ever passing my lips."

"I think you *mean* well," Kim replied. "But there's obviously something upsetting Kiran, and Rocky's not at all sensitive. It could be the biggest mistake you've ever made."

"Oh, zip it," I retorted sulkily, following Kiran out of the classroom. Whoever would have thought the day would come when *Kim* would be lecturing *me*? Oh, for the good old days when I was in charge . . .

Once outside, I steered Kiran and Kim over to the wall by the canteen. It was a see-and-be-seen kind of place, so there was no chance that Rocky would miss us. And no chance that I would miss him. I had a secret suspicion that he wouldn't be at all keen to put his side of the deal into practice, and I was determined to make sure that he did.

At first there was no sign of him. Kim and I chatted idly about homework, while Kiran sat there in silence. After a few moments, Jazz joined us.

"Oh, so you're still here, Amber," she giggled. "I thought you might have left the country."

"Ha ha," I said curtly. "Leave Auntie and Auntie-ji to me."

"Are you in trouble or something?" Kiran asked.

"Not at all," I replied as Jazz sniggered some more.

Just then Rocky came out of school. He was chatting to Geena, and both of them happened to glance in our direction. Rocky's face fell down to his knees. It was extremely difficult to glare at someone so beautiful, but I just about managed it.

Sulkily Rocky made his way over to us, his feet (in, naturally, very expensive trainers) dragging on the ground. Geena didn't look too pleased, either, to have their cozy little chat interrupted.

"Hello, Rocky," I said, indicating Kiran with the tiniest nod of my head.

"Hi." Rocky cleared his throat. "Hello, Kiran."

Kiran was so surprised, she almost fell off the wall. "Oh—h-hello," she stuttered.

I stared hard at Rocky, willing him on.

"Look, I'm sorry about Saturday," he muttered, sounding as if every word was being pulled from him by force. "It's just that I've been looking for that CD for ages."

"So have I," said Kiran. She smiled a little. She looked so much better when she smiled. "I've got everything JC's ever done."

"Me too." Rocky frowned. "Well, almost."

There was a short pause, and then they both laughed. I beamed. So did Geena and Jazz. Even Kim was smiling. Who was the idiot who said my ideas never work?

Rocky and Kiran were chatting about their favorite bhangra bands.

"I'm into the Punjabi Punks in a big way," Rocky was saying. "And have you heard that new guy, Harbinder? 'Bhangra Nights' is a brilliant track."

"That's not Harbinder," Kiran said with a frown. "'Bhangra Nights' is by Desi MC."

Rocky shook his head. "No, it isn't."

"Yes, it is," Kiran contradicted him coolly.

Rocky stared at her. I shifted uneasily. I was beginning to sense trouble in what might have been paradise.

"You're wrong," Rocky snapped.

"No, *you're* wrong," Kiran said quietly but firmly.

Rocky's face turned red. "We'll see!" he growled, and stomped off.

"Well." Kiran raised her eyebrows at me. She didn't look at all upset. "He's touchy, isn't he?"

"I told you this wouldn't work," Kim said self-righteously as we went back into school. Kiran had gone ahead of us, totally unmoved by Rocky's temper tantrum.

"Yes, Amber," Jazz chimed in. "You've just made things worse."

"You traitor," I said bitterly. "You said it was good psychology."

"No, that was Geena," Jazz replied. "I agreed with her, but I had my doubts."

I was secretly beginning to have my *own* doubts. Could Rocky pull this off? I wasn't convinced. But, of course, I still had one ace up my sleeve.

I reminded Rocky of this when I managed to corner him in the library during the afternoon.

"What are you playing at with Kiran?" I demanded. "Do you want this gig at my aunt's wedding or not?"

"Yeah, course I do," Rocky replied sullenly. "It's just that Kiran really winds me up."

"Well, get it sorted," I said coldly. "You and Kiran have got to be best mates by the wedding, or our deal's off."

"OK, OK," Rocky muttered. "Look, I'll check out who's right when I get home tonight. Once I've proved her wrong, she'll have to apologize and I can take it from there."

"You're very confident," I said.

"Hey." Rocky winked at me. "I am DJ Rocket Man, after all."

"Pardon?"

"DJ Rocket Man." Rocky puffed out his chest proudly. "That's my performing name."

"Er—lovely," I said. "Now don't forget. I want to see some results."

Rocky slid his arm round my shoulders and gave me a squeeze. "No problem, gorgeous," he whispered in my ear. Which sent me on my way, smiling.

Oh, I was feeling very pleased with myself. At the end of the day, while I waited in the playground for Geena and Jazz, I mentally ticked off the things I was pleased about, and which I'd had a definite hand in. One: Auntie and Mr. Arora were getting married. Two: Rocky was going to cheer Kiran up, which would put me in Mr. Arora's good books and, therefore, in Auntie's. Three: I was becoming more and more convinced that Rocky liked me best, after that little display in the school library. However, the only fly in the ointment was—

"Where's Kim?" asked Jazz, wandering out of the lower-school doors. "Isn't she walking home with us?"

"No, thank the Lord," I replied. "She left early to go to the dentist. Hopefully he'll tell her to stop talking so much or her teeth will fall out."

Jazz chuckled. "Has she been giving you earache about Kiran?"

"Oh, yes," I sighed as we joined up with Geena at the gates. "She's full of it. She's totally stressing me out."

"Talking of stress," Geena broke in, frowning, "has either of you noticed how hassled Mr. Arora's been looking lately?"

Jazz and I looked blank.

"Not really," I replied.

"We had him for maths today," Geena went on. "He was in a right mood. He nearly ripped Damon Keating's head off for getting a couple of sums wrong."

"That doesn't sound like Mr. Arora," I said. "Maybe he's finding the job of head of the lower school a bit difficult. There must be a lot of paperwork."

Geena shook her head. "I reckon there's more to it than that," she said solemnly. "I think all this wedding stuff with Auntie and Auntie-ji is getting to him."

"And talking of that," Jazz said gleefully, "we still have the prospect of Amber telling the aunties about Rocky to look forward to."

"Oh, dear," I said, with my nose in the air. "Your life must be *very* boring if that's so interesting to you."

I was doing my very best to be brave. But when we arrived home and saw Auntie-ji's white BMW parked at the curb, it took all my iron self-control not to freak out right there and then.

"You might as well tell them now," Geena remarked with evident enjoyment as she slotted her key into the front door, "seeing as they're both here."

"Oh, yes," agreed Jazz. "It's the perfect opportunity."

"Of course," I replied coolly, while at the same time feeling as if I'd left my stomach behind on the front doorstep. Like a dead woman walking, I followed Geena and Jazz into the sitting room.

"Hello, girls!" Auntie-ji boomed, leaping to her feet

and beginning the usual round of bone-crushing embraces. "How are you?"

Auntie looked mightily pleased to see us too. I guessed that Auntie-ji had only just arrived, and we'd saved Auntie from having to entertain her on her own.

"Amber's got something to tell you," Jazz announced when Auntie-ji had put her down and retreated to the sofa again.

"No, I haven't," I said quickly.

"Yes, you have," said Geena and Jazz together.

I was therefore forced to rely on the lightning-quick responses of my brilliant brain.

"Actually, I *have* got something to say," I began. I turned to Auntie-ji. "Geena, Jazz and I were wondering if you'd like to come shopping with us tomorrow."

Geena and Jazz both gasped in horror, but luckily they were drowned out by Auntie-ji's scream of joy.

"I'd love to!" she proclaimed, her round face beaming with utter happiness. "I'm sure we'll find some lovely wedding outfits for you this time."

Geena and Jazz were shooting poisonous glares at me. Auntie, on the other hand, merely looked suspicious.

"Amber, will you come and help me make tea, please?" she asked.

"Of course," I replied cheerfully.

Phase Two of my plan to avert catastrophe. I strolled jauntily into the kitchen, leaving Auntie-ji pinching Jazz's cheeks playfully.

"What's going on?" Auntie demanded, filling the kettle.

"What do you mean?" I asked with wide-eyed amazement.

"I thought the four of us were going shopping together tomorrow," Auntie went on. "I know you were looking forward to it. You're up to something, Ambajit Dhillon, and I want to know what it is."

"We just thought that we'd get Auntie-ji out of your hair for a bit," I said casually. "You know, give you some time for yourself."

Auntie looked stunned. "Oh!"

"You've been looking a bit tense lately," I went on. "So has Mr. Arora. We just wanted to make sure that everything was all right."

"I'm touched," said Auntie. "Thank you very much."

Now or never. I cleared my throat. "There is one other thing. . . ."

Auntie threw her eyes up to heaven. "I knew it!" But she was smiling, which gave me courage. "What is it?"

"I've organized the music for your wedding party," I said in a rush.

Auntie stopped smiling. "You have?"

Quickly I explained about Rocky, although I didn't tell her about our deal. "He's really into bhangra, and I'm sure he'll be a fab DJ," I said pleadingly. "And he writes all his own songs."

Auntie frowned. "He's really fit, too, isn't he?" she added.

I stared at her in disbelief.

"I heard you three discussing him last week," she said with a grin. She shrugged. "Oh, well, why not? I shall enjoy telling Auntie-ji that we've already arranged the music for the party. Last week she was talking about hiring a symphony orchestra."

I gave a sigh of relief and picked up the tea tray. "So that's all right, then?"

Auntie nodded. "You know, Amber, you're getting quite skillful at interfering," she remarked.

"Well, I *was* taught by the master," I retorted.

We were laughing as we went back into the living room. Geena and Jazz were looking completely disgruntled. Auntie-ji was in the middle of a long and boring story about her childhood in Slough.

"Oh, Auntie-ji, we have something to tell you," Auntie said casually as she poured the tea. "Amber has arranged the music for the wedding party."

I couldn't resist glancing at Geena and Jazz. Their eyes were practically out on stalks, and you could have driven an express train through their open mouths. Meanwhile, Auntie-ji was looking enormously disappointed.

"Who will be playing?" she asked glumly.

Auntie explained about Rocky, while Jazz and Geena stared at me in disbelief. They couldn't believe I'd got away with it. To be honest, neither could I.

"Oh." Auntie-ji seemed so very depressed, I couldn't help feeling just a tiny bit guilty. "Well, don't worry. I'm sure I can cancel."

"You mean you'd already booked something?" asked Auntie, trying not to sound accusing.

Auntie-ji nodded. "You remember the Bhangra Boyz?"

Geena, Jazz and I looked blank, but Auntie gasped.

"My very favorite pop band of the eighties!" she said with a sigh. "I loved them to bits." She stared at Auntie-ji. "You can't have booked them. They split up years ago."

"I persuaded them to get back together for your wedding party," Auntie-ji explained. "Most of them live in the UK, but we were going to fly the drummer and the bass player over from India."

"Oh!" Auntie sank into the nearest armchair, looking overwhelmed.

I began to feel extremely uncomfortable. Meanwhile, Geena and Jazz were obviously enjoying the high drama.

Auntie-ji tapped a fingernail thoughtfully against one of her gold teeth. "Perhaps Amber's friend and the band could both perform," she suggested. "After all, it would be nice to have a local boy as part of the entertainment. That way we'd get the best of both worlds."

"Amber?" Auntie stared hopefully at me.

"Of course," I agreed weakly. I couldn't believe I'd got off so lightly with both of them. But I was a bit worried that Rocky might think I'd broken our deal. I decided there and then that I wouldn't tell him he would be sharing the limelight until the very last minute.

"You have got to be the luckiest person in this entire world, Amber," Jazz whispered in a disappointed voice as the tea was finally poured. "I really thought you were going to die."

"Yes, and we were so looking forward to it," Geena added.

I smiled smugly. "Stick with me, kids, and you'll learn a lot," I replied with a wink.

However, my luck finally ran out on Saturday when Auntie-ji turned up at 8:55 sharp to take us shopping. I realized, with a sinking heart, that it was a heavy price to pay for not getting into trouble over Rocky and the wedding party.

"Do you want to strangle Amber, Jazz," asked Geena as we trudged down the Broadway behind Auntie-ji, "or shall I do it?"

"You do it," Jazz muttered. "Your hands are bigger than mine, and it'll be a more painful death."

"Look, how many more times do I have to say I'm sorry?" I demanded. We'd just suffered another lengthy session in Sameera's shop and had only just escaped by the skin of our teeth from being forced to buy the wedding outfits from fashion hell.

"Well, let's see," said Geena. "About ten million should do it."

We had stopped for the fourth time so that Auntie-ji could greet one of her many acquaintances. Once again, we had to endure the usual round of hugs, cheek pinching, head patting and questions about school. We were on our way to Jyoti Fashions, which was second only to Sameera's in complete non-hipness.

"Oh, come on," I argued. "She's not that bad."

"No," agreed Geena with heavy sarcasm. "She'd be lovely if she just shut up for a moment or two and listened to what we said instead of ignoring us."

"This is going to be terrible," Jazz muttered. "Oh, it's so not fair of you to drag us into this, Amber. . . ."

She and Geena grumbled on while Auntie-ji chatted to her friend. I wasn't listening to either of them. My eye had been caught by a poster written in various Asian languages and in English, which was pinned in the window of Jaffa's sweet shop.

THE NAYA ZINDAGI DROP-IN COMMUNITY CENTER NEEDS **YOU!**

WE ARE DESPERATELY SEARCHING FOR VOLUNTEERS
TO KEEP OUR CENTER OPEN.
CAN YOU HELP OUT WITH MOTHER AND BABY GROUPS?
DELIVER HOT MEALS TO THE ELDERLY?
RUN FUND-RAISING EVENTS?
EVEN IF YOU CAN ONLY MAKE TEA, WE WANT TO MEET YOU!
PLEASE POP INTO THE CENTER TO SAY HELLO.
WE ARE IN SHEPHERD ROAD, JUST AROUND
THE CORNER FROM THIS SHOP.

Though I say it myself, my brain was really working at lightning speed these days. The ideas were coming thick and fast! The minute Auntie-ji said goodbye to her friend, I took her arm and dragged her over to the window.

"Look at this, Auntie-ji."

"Yes, I've heard of them," Auntie-ji replied, putting on her glasses to read the poster. "They do very good work in our community."

"They're looking for volunteers," I said pointedly.

"Yes, I would imagine they're always short of people," Auntie-ji said, popping her glasses back in her handbag. "Now, shall we go to Jyoti Fashions?"

I sighed. Why was it that no one else could keep up with me?

"Why don't *you* volunteer?" I suggested.

"Me!" Auntie-ji's eyebrows shot upward. "But I never have a minute to spare. I'm far too busy."

"Well, they always say if you want something done, ask a busy person to do it," I reminded her.

"Yes . . ." Auntie-ji stared thoughtfully at the poster. "Maybe I'll pop in sometime for a chat."

"Why don't you go right now?" I suggested ruthlessly. I pointed in the direction of Shepherd Road. "It's just there. We'll have a look in the shops around here."

"Well, all right," Auntie-ji agreed. "I won't be long. But don't bother going into Kareena's. The clothes in there are really outrageous."

We watched her turn down Shepherd Road, and then we dived straight through the door of Kareena's.

"You know, Amber," Jazz said grudgingly, "sometimes your ideas aren't half bad."

"Thank you," I replied. "I'm on a roll at the moment, as you might have noticed."

"Hi, girls," said Lakshmi, the shop owner. She was tall and slim, with dyed red hair, a silver nose ring and Jimmy Choo shoes. "Long time no see."

"We need some outfits for our aunt's wedding," I explained. "Anything brown and sack-like is definitely off-limits."

"And hurry," Geena added.

However, Auntie-ji was a very long time. We'd all chosen our outfits by the time she peered through the shop window, looking for us. We'd even had time for a lengthy argument with Jazz about the revealing side splits in the skirt she'd chosen.

"Sorry I was so long, girls," Auntie-ji panted. She was pink in the face with excitement. "There was so much to discuss."

"So are you going to volunteer?" I asked eagerly.

Auntie-ji nodded. "I'm going to help with the mum and baby group on Monday afternoon. See how I get on."

Geena and Jazz looked at me admiringly, and I felt very pleased with myself. I was sure that if Auntie-ji had something else to think about, she wouldn"t interfere quite so much with the wedding. I was also sure that Auntie and Mr. Arora would be very grateful. Oh, why couldn't everyone be as clever as me?

"So you've chosen your outfits, then." Auntie-ji noted the clothes we were carrying with slight disapproval.

"And for you?" Lakshmi hurried toward Auntie-ji

on her five-inch heels. "I have a lilac suit embroidered with gold that would suit you perfectly."

"Oh!" Auntie-ji looked quite shocked as Lakshmi whisked the suit off a rail. "I never usually wear those kinds of colors." She fingered the thin, silky material. "But it *is* lovely. . . ."

"Try it on," urged Geena.

"Oh, all right." Auntie-ji beamed at us. "No harm in living dangerously for once, is there, girls?"

Auntie-ji bought the lilac suit. Then she treated us to an eat-all-you-like lunch at the Curry Queen, at four pounds a head. Afterward we went home, where Auntie and Mr. Arora both looked pleased and relieved to hear that Auntie-ji had found something else to do other than interfere with their wedding. I also made sure that Auntie knew it was my idea. She thanked me, but she had something else to say too.

"Don't forget, Amber," she said wisely, "the art of interfering is knowing exactly when to stop."

Oh, why, why, *why* didn't I listen to her?

chapter 8

I was rushing headlong toward disaster, but by the beginning of the following week, I hadn't realized it yet. In fact, things were still going swimmingly.

First, Rocky turned up at school on Monday morning, precisely one minute before the bell rang, with a face of the darkest thunder.

"Let me guess," I said instantly. "Kiran was right and you were wrong about that bhangra track."

Rocky flushed deep red. "I don't know how I made a mistake," he muttered. "I must have been having an off day."

"That's all right," I told him. "I'm sure Kiran won't hold it against you if you apologize right away."

"*Apologize?*" Rocky gasped, as shocked as if I'd ordered him to kiss Mr. Grimwade.

"Well, yes," I replied. "You *do* remember the deal?"

Rocky stared glumly at his expensive trainers (a different pair this time). "I'll do it later," he mumbled. "There isn't time before the bell."

"It only takes two seconds to say you're sorry." I gave him a little push toward Kiran, who was sitting on the wall with a book. "Off you go."

"I don't know how you're getting away with this, Amber," Geena remarked as Rocky trudged off, "but all your ideas seem to be working splendidly."

"At the moment," Jazz added darkly.

"Well, she was bound to hit a lucky streak at some point," Kim observed. "But it can't last forever."

"You three can insult me all you like," I said haughtily. "I'm not in this for the praise and glory. I just like helping people."

"And you fancy Rocky," Geena added. "That's a big incentive."

We watched Rocky approach Kiran. I think he managed to force out an apology, but it took a great deal of effort. They chatted for a moment before the bell rang. Then they smiled at each other—actually *smiled*—before going their separate ways.

"Watch and learn from the queen of the good idea," I told Geena, Jazz and Kim smugly as I strolled toward the lower-school entrance. Sadly, the effect was spoilt a little when I tripped over my trailing shoelace. They all sniggered as my nose headed straight toward the floor, but luckily someone caught my arm just before I made contact.

"It's OK, Amber," said George with a grin. "You don't have to fall at my feet every time you see me."

"Very amusing," I said coldly, pulling myself free.

George cocked an eyebrow at me. "Thank you, George. Don't mention it, Amber."

"I was just coming to that," I snapped. "Thank you."

George followed me into the lower school. Jazz and Kim hurried along behind us, ears flapping.

"When you get fed up with old Bighead," George went on, "I'll still be here."

"Bighead?" I repeated, pretending I didn't know whom he meant.

George roared with laughter while I stared crossly at him. "You know who. He's a loser."

"I think not," I said, as coolly as I could.

George shrugged. "Still trying to win the bet, then?"

I stopped dead, and Kim and Jazz thudded heavily into the back of me.

"How do you know about the bet?" I demanded.

George tapped me teasingly on the nose. "I have my ways," he said with glee, and sauntered away.

"Right!" I snapped. "Only four people know about this bet. Me, Geena, Jazz and—"

I stared hard at Kim, who had gone crimson.

"I didn't think it was a secret," she said, trying to sound assertive instead of guilty.

"It isn't." I scowled. "But I expect a bit more loyalty from my friends."

"If it's not a secret," Kim replied, "then I haven't been disloyal."

"There are different ways of being disloyal," I countered.

"So was it a secret or wasn't it?"

Jazz groaned. "This conversation is killing me," she muttered, wandering off toward the Year 8 classrooms.

"Look," said Kim, "George asked me if you liked Rocky, so I told him about the bet. End of story."

"That was a mistake," I said crossly. "You should have kept your mouth shut."

"Does it matter?" asked Kim as we walked into the classroom. "No one else knows."

"Amber!" Chelsea Dixon screeched across the room. "Is it true that you, Geena and Jazz have made a bet to see which one of you Rocky Gill likes best?"

The whole class cheered as I blushed.

"My money's on you, Amber," said Mr. Hernandez, who was engaged in his daily task of searching for the register.

"Is that true?" Kiran asked me as I sank into my chair and tried to make myself invisible.

"Oh, it's just a bit of fun," I said in an offhand tone.

Kiran said no more. I didn't think anything of that at the time.

It only began to make sense later. . . .

"I want a word with you, Ambajit Dhillon." Jazz stomped across the playground toward me, fury radiating from every pore. "The whole of Year Eight is talking about our bet!"

"Our year too." Geena flew toward me from the

opposite corner of the playground like an avenging fury. "Rocky must have heard about it by now. It's totally embarrassing."

I pointed at Kim. "Blame Miss Blabbermouth here."

Kim looked unconcerned. "Rocky already guessed what you were up to. I told you that before."

"You can't know that for sure," Geena retorted.

"I do," Kim argued. "He always has a smug look on his face when he talks to you three."

"Can I just suggest that you stop interfering in other people's business," I said in a freezing tone.

"Ha!" Kim exclaimed scornfully. "That's a joke, coming from you."

"I don't interfere," I said. "I help people. That's the difference. See?"

I pointed across the playground. Rocky and Kiran were walking slowly toward the school. Their heads were close together, and they were having what looked like a very deep discussion.

"Like *that's* not going to end in tears," Kim said in a doom-laden voice.

We ignored her and left to join Rocky and Kiran. They were arguing about music, but in a good-humored way. They were both laughing.

"Hey, girls." Rocky gave us a slow, deliberate wink, which left me in no doubt at all that he knew about the bet. "Sorry, haven't got time to chat at the moment."

"Why not?" demanded Jazz.

"Mr. Fowler wants volunteers to help him tidy the

music room," Rocky replied. "So I asked Kiran to give me a hand."

"Let me get this straight," I said. "You two are giving up part of your lunch hour to help the head of the music department tidy up?"

Kiran grinned. "Not just that," she said. "I reckon Rocky here thinks that if he gets in Mr. Fowler's good books, he might be asked to DJ at the next school disco!"

"Yeah, why not?" Rocky retorted. "I'm the best." And the two of them started laughing again.

"I see," I said. "Do you want any more help?"

"Nah, we're good, thanks." Rocky raised a hand at us. "Catch you later."

They went into the upper-school entrance, and we were left outside like starving urchins with our noses pressed up against a baker's window. It did not feel good to watch Kiran waltzing off with the best-looking boy in the school. I knew Rocky was only hanging out with her because it was part of the deal. But *still* . . .

"They seem to be getting on well," I muttered sulkily.

"At least Rocky's keeping his part of the bargain," Geena said, looking no better pleased herself.

"Yes, but how are we supposed to keep this bet going if he's spending all his time with Kiran?" Jazz wanted to know.

"Patience," I replied. "This is only a temporary blip. We watch and we wait."

So we watched and we waited. That week, things appeared to be going as wonderfully as even I could have wished for. Kiran and Rocky met up whenever they could to talk about music, swap CDs, borrow each other's MP3 players and generally have what looked like a very good time of it. Kiran had started to look a lot more relaxed. And within a few days everyone in the school had started to notice that she and Rocky were becoming rather matey mates.

"So what's Kiran got that you, Jazz and Geena haven't?" asked Chelsea Dixon, quite offensively, on seeing Kiran and Rocky fooling around one break time.

"An in-depth knowledge of bhangra and hip-hop," I retorted. "And that is all."

"They look very cozy together," observed Sharelle Alexander. "Are they in *love*?"

I laughed long and hard. "Don't be ridiculous," I said coolly. "They're just friends."

And, of course, George Botley had to stick his oar in too, didn't he.

"Has Lover Boy found someone else, then, Amber?" he inquired with a grin. "Never mind. You've still got me."

"Now why does that make me feel like slitting my throat?" I replied.

George laughed uproariously. "You can mock—" he began.

"Thanks, I will," I broke in.

"But you'll see I'm right eventually," George went on. "You'll soon get fed up with Rocky Gill. He's not your type."

"And you are?" I asked with more than a touch of scorn.

"Yep." George nodded. "Rocky's an idiot."

I did not reply to that. Rocky was no idiot, but a tiny part of me—a teeny, weeny part—knew that otherwise George was absolutely right.

I mean, you couldn't expect someone as stunningly good-looking as Rocky to have a personality to match, could you? That would be totally unfair and against all the laws of nature.

Oh, Rocky was beautiful, yes indeed. But he wasn't exactly the sharpest knife in the drawer. Geena was in all the top sets in her year, and Rocky wasn't in *any* of her classes. He was nice enough. He just wasn't Mr. Charisma. He was very self-absorbed, in himself and in his music. That didn't make him a bad person. But it did make him a not-very-interesting one.

So did that mean I was giving up on the bet? Are you *crazy*? I was more determined than ever to win it and show Geena and Jazz exactly who was the boss around here! And anyway, I was still enjoying feasting my eyes on Rocky whenever the occasion arose.

But I should have guessed that trouble was just around the corner. . . .

The bubble finally burst at the end of the week. Geena, Jazz and I were wandering on our merry way to school, feeling quite calm and at peace with the world. Well, I was. Geena and Jazz were moaning, as ever.

"It's impossible to get near Rocky these days," Geena grumbled, "what with Kiran sticking to him like glue."

"I vote we declare this bet null and void," Jazz complained.

I raised my eyebrows. "Scared of losing?"

"Not at all," Jazz shot back. "But like Geena said, it's impossible."

"You two are never happy," I sighed. "Mr. Arora landed us with looking after Kiran. I sorted that out. I got Auntie-ji fixed up at the community center. Which, may I remind you, calmed *our* auntie down and made life at home a lot more bearable."

"I'll give you that," Geena said grudgingly.

Auntie-ji had popped in for five minutes early one morning, just to see how the wedding arrangements were coming along, with just over two weeks to go. But she hadn't stayed long because she was taking a party of pensioners to the seaside. She had bounced out of the house, looking as happy as Larry, whoever he might be.

"That reminds me," Jazz said, with the air of one who was determined to stir it. "What's going to happen after the wedding?"

I looked blank. "Auntie and Mr. Arora are going to live happily ever after, I suppose," I replied.

"No, I meant Rocky and Kiran," said Jazz impatiently. "He's only being friendly with her because you made that deal. Is he going to drop her like a hot potato after the wedding?"

"Ooh, good point," Geena agreed. "Amber?"

"Of course not," I blustered. "I think Rocky has actually discovered that he really does like Kiran. All right, so he's never going to fall madly in love with her, but they'll stay mates."

Geena and Jazz both looked disappointed.

"I could bang your heads together," I grumbled. "You complain when my ideas don't work, and then you don't like it when they *do*."

Geena and Jazz were now grinning like two idiots.

"What?" I asked, looking round.

Rocky was walking down the road toward us. Did I say walk? *Stamp* would describe it better. Or *stomp*. Anyway, he looked very angry. But still beautiful, of course.

"Hello, Rocky," Geena said in a Marilyn Monroe breathy voice. "Don't you usually get a lift to school?"

"Yeah, I do," Rocky growled sulkily. "Only my daft mother has gone and pranged the side of the Merc. It's gone to be fixed. Dad's away on business and he's got the BMW. So I've got to walk."

"Well, it's nice to see you—" I began, elbowing Jazz neatly into the gutter to get beside him.

Rocky ignored me. "We've got the van, but Mum won't drive it. Which is probably a good thing. She'd only smash it up, anyway." He scowled. "Women drivers!"

Jazz frowned. I bit down on my lip. Geena wasn't going to let that go, however. Not even for the sake of a slave-for-the-day bet.

"What do you mean?" she said.

"You know." Rocky shrugged. "They're always driving into things."

"So your dad's never bumped into anything?" Geena asked coolly.

"Well, yeah, once or twice," muttered Rocky.

Geena was going for the kill. "How many times?"

I think Rocky was just starting to realize that Geena wasn't too happy when something happened that grabbed our attention. We turned the corner, and there at the other end of the street we saw Kim and Kiran.

They were standing in the road, facing up to two boys who wore the uniform of Grange Street School, Coppergate's biggest enemy. The boys were older, and one of them was even taller than Kiran. It seemed as if they were arguing.

"What's going on?" I asked.

"Looks like trouble," said Rocky.

I half expected him to race down the road ahead of us like some superhero. He didn't.

We hurried toward them. But before we got there, the two boys turned and walked off, making rude gestures as they went.

"Are you OK?" I rushed up to Kim and Kiran. Kim was looking quite pale and shaken, and I put my arm round her. "What happened?"

"I was on my way to school early to go to the library," Kim gulped, "and those two boys grabbed my bag and threw it into the tree." She pointed upward.

Kiran was already climbing the tree to get it. She retrieved Kim's rucksack from the branch where it was lying, and climbed neatly down again.

"Where did you learn to do *that*?" asked Jazz, mouth open wide.

"I was a monkey in a previous life," Kiran said with a grin. She handed the rucksack to Kim. "There you go."

Kim took the rucksack and hugged it to her. "Kiran came along and saved me," she said shakily. "I asked those boys—assertively—to leave me alone. But they wouldn't."

I stared at Kiran. "That was brave," I said. "One of them was built like the Incredible Hulk."

Kiran shrugged. "It was nothing."

"Shame we didn't turn up a bit earlier," said Rocky. "I'd soon have sorted them out."

"Yeah, I'm sure you would have," Kiran replied with a little smile.

I was still staring at her. Changes had been happening over the last few weeks, which I was only just noticing. Her cropped hair had grown and it was curling all over her head now. She looked smarter and generally a bit more together. And was that a touch of lip gloss she was wearing?

I watched Kiran smiling at Rocky. Those weren't the only changes. There was a sparkle in her eyes and a spring in her step.

And suddenly it hit me with all the force of a speeding train.

Had Kiran gone and fallen for the very obvious charms of Rocky Gill?

chapter 9

We walked the rest of the way to school together, but I didn't speak to or look at anyone. I was in a daze, a haze of guilt.

I'd pushed Kiran toward Rocky. Now she'd fallen head over heels for him—and there was absolutely no chance of him feeling the same way. I'd made the situation one million times worse. . . .

"You're very quiet, Amber," said Geena suspiciously as we got closer to school.

"Is that a crime?" I retorted. "Can't a girl have a bit of time to meditate and be quiet within herself for five minutes?"

Geena stared hard at me. "Oh, now I know for a fact that there's something wrong," she said. "You're never quiet, Amber."

"You even talk in your sleep," added Jazz.

"Shhh!" I jerked my head toward Rocky and Kiran, who were walking in front of us. "I don't want them to hear."

"We're going to the shop to get some chocolate," Rocky called, turning round. "Do you girls want anything?"

I shook my head. "We'll carry on to school," I called. "See you later."

"Right, what's going on?" demanded Geena as we hurried away.

"I'm a fool," I said tragically.

"So what's new?" Jazz yawned. "I thought it was something serious."

"This *is* serious," I snapped. "Do you know what I think? I think Kiran's in love with Rocky."

Geena, Jazz and Kim stopped dead and stared at me.

"Oh no," Geena breathed. "You *are* joking? No, on second thought it makes perfect sense."

"He's going to break her heart," predicted Jazz dolefully. "I knew you shouldn't have interfered, Amber."

"Has Kiran told you so?" Kim asked.

"No," I replied, "but it's obvious. Just take a look at her."

Kim was shaking her head. "Rocky's not Kiran's type," she said. "She's clever and funny. Rocky's not that intelligent, and he can be a bit dull."

It was interesting that neither I, Geena nor Jazz leaped to Rocky's defense, as we would have done before.

"But Kiran has changed over the last couple of weeks," I persisted. "You have to admit that."

"Maybe she's just settling in at last," replied Kim. "And she might have started to deal with her father's death too."

The three of us stared at Kim.

"How do you know about that?" I demanded.

"She told me one day last week," Kim said casually. "We had quite a long chat."

"Well, you're a dark horse, aren't you." I felt somewhat annoyed. "You never said."

Kim grinned. "You're not the only one who can keep a secret," she retorted.

"So what are you going to do now, Amber?" asked Jazz. "Are you going to talk to Kiran?"

"No, she isn't," said Geena and Kim together.

"Why not?" I muttered. "I got her into this mess. I'll have to get her out of it."

"I think you've done quite enough," Geena said sternly. "Leave it. You'll only make things worse."

"But it was me who forced Rocky to make friends with her in the first place," I said hopelessly. "Now she's in love with him, and he's only using her because he wants to play at Auntie's wedding. He might not even want to be friends with her afterward. How is she going to feel?"

Geena, Kim and Jazz stared at me in silence. When it was summed up like that, it sounded truly appalling.

"Surely Rocky couldn't be so insensitive and unfeeling," said Geena cautiously.

Kim, Jazz and I didn't say anything. It was painfully obvious that not a single one of us had much faith in Rocky's ability to handle a delicate emotional situation.

Now, I wasn't going to tell the others this, but I did have a plan. If it wasn't a good idea to talk to Kiran (and I could see that maybe it wasn't), that didn't stop me talking to Rocky and trying to find out if his intentions were honorable.

I'm aware this is very strange. You might tell me I was wrong, but *honestly*, I didn't think I was. I believed that Rocky might—just *might*—have gone and fallen for Kiran himself!

I know it sounds ridiculous. I know I might have been fooling myself. And, truthfully, I didn't believe it to begin with. But all the signs pointed that way.

I spent the next few days trying to get Rocky on his own so I could have a word with him. Same old problem. If he wasn't talking music with Kiran, Geena and Jazz were forever hanging around, still determined to win the bet. To be perfectly frank, the bet was the last thing on my mind. But what happened was that I did start noticing exactly how Rocky treated Kiran.

He was nice to her. Sweet, even. He shared his chocolate bars with her. He brought her CDs to borrow. He looked out for her in the playground at every opportunity. He spent a lot of time chatting with her. He was certainly going far beyond the friendliness that our deal required.

"Could it be possible?" I asked myself, time and time again. "*Is* it possible?"

And the answer I came up with was—why not?

I dared to dream. And besides, it would get me very neatly off the hook. . . .

"You were right, you know, Amber," Jazz said solemnly. We were sitting on the canteen wall one lunchtime the following week, watching Rocky and Kiran making their way slowly across the playground toward us. "Kiran's in love with Rocky, and from here on in, that can only mean heartbreak and agony. And it's all your fault."

"Not necessarily," I said.

Geena, Jazz and Kim looked surprised.

"What do you mean?" asked Geena.

"Look more closely," I told them. "Can't you see what's going on before your very eyes?"

They all stared obediently at Rocky and Kiran, who had stopped to look at a couple of CDs Kiran had taken from her bag.

"No," they said together.

"Kiran and Rocky," I explained impatiently. "It isn't all one-way traffic."

"What have cars got to do with anything?" Jazz began, but Geena interrupted her.

"Oh, really, Amber!" she snapped, looking quite angry. "You're not suggesting—? That's ridiculous!"

"You think so?" Kim nodded several times. "I can believe that, actually. Amber could be right."

"Will someone please tell me what's going on?" Jazz screeched.

"It's absurd, but now Amber thinks *Rocky* fancies *Kiran*," Geena said curtly.

Jazz glared at us. "Stop messing about and tell me what's *really* going on."

"That's it," I replied.

Jazz stared at me incredulously, then she burst out laughing.

"What's so funny?" I asked.

"Well, *look* at Kiran!" Jazz began. "Look at *us*." She stopped, suddenly realizing that she was getting into deep waters.

"Go on," I said.

Jazz blushed. "Do I have to?"

"You might as well," Kim said. "It's what the three of you are thinking, anyway."

"We're not all as shallow as Jazz," Geena retorted.

"I'm not shallow," Jazz said crossly. "Oh, all right, then. What I mean is that Kiran isn't even pretty, and we're all much better-looking. Even Amber."

"Thank you for that vote of confidence," I said. "But haven't you heard of the old saying that what's on the inside matters more than what's on the outside?"

"Yes, but I don't believe it," Jazz replied. "Not where boys are concerned."

"Me neither," added Geena. "Not in this case, anyway. Especially since you and Rocky made that deal. He'd do anything to play at Auntie's wedding."

"Well, I think Amber could be right," Kim broke in. "I bet Rocky's never met such an interesting girl as Kiran, even if it *was* only because Amber blackmailed him. I expect most of the females who hang around him are shallow, empty-headed bimbos."

"I hope you're not referring to anyone in particular," Jazz said with a glare.

"And don't think we haven't noticed that if it *is* true, it would get you out of a tricky situation, Amber," Geena said sternly.

"Would it?" Jazz looked blank. "How?"

Geena cast up her eyes. "It would mean a nice, neat happy ending, and no heartbreak for Kiran."

"Oh, I see." Jazz grinned at me. "So Amber's imagining things because she feels desperately guilty?"

"Right," Geena said. "And I, for one, think it's a complete load of nonsense—"

Kiran dropped one of the CDs. Rocky bent to pick it up. He slid his arm round her waist and gave her a squeeze. Kiran laughed. She pushed him away. They began to mock-wrestle in the way that people who fancy each other (but haven't admitted it) often do.

"Still think I'm making it up?" I asked triumphantly.

Geena and Jazz looked visibly shocked.

"I can't believe it," Jazz muttered. "I *won't* believe it."

"I suppose it *might* be true," said Geena weakly.

"If it is, she'd better let him win the fight," Jazz whispered. At the moment Kiran had Rocky in an armlock and showed no sign of letting go.

"I thought he said he couldn't fancy anyone whose hands were bigger than his," Geena said grumpily.

"Obviously he's changed his mind," I replied. "We'll just have to live with it."

"I know it's a big blow to your enormous egos," said Kim kindly, "but you could try to be happy for Kiran."

Jazz gulped. "I suppose so," she said through gritted teeth.

"I guess this means our bet is off," muttered Geena.

"There doesn't seem to be much point to it now, does there?" I agreed sadly.

Kiran had won when she hadn't even known about the bet in the first place. . . .

While it seemed that romance was brewing between Kiran and Rocky, we also had a love affair closer to home to look forward to. With only a week to go to the wedding, the kurmai, Mr. Arora and Auntie's engagement party, was held on Saturday.

"I think it's about time we stopped calling him Mr. Arora, don't you?" Geena observed sensibly as we fought to get our share of chicken and dhal. We were crammed into the Aroras' living room, along with assorted relatives from both sides of the family, and there was a desperate scrum for food. We were sandwiched between large, chattering aunties and bawling kids, and however hard we shoved, we didn't seem to be getting any closer to the table.

"It seems like tempting fate to start calling him Uncle before they actually get married," I replied.

"What are we going to call him when we're at school?" Jazz demanded. She ducked under an auntie's elbow and snared a samosa. "He can't be Uncle there."

"Well, *hello*," said Geena. "We carry on calling him Mr. Arora, of course."

"Surely even your tiny brain can cope with him having one name at school and another at home, Jazz," I scoffed.

Jazz looked affronted and ate the samosa without even offering us a bite. Meanwhile, Auntie, looking very sweet and innocent, was sitting on the sofa with Mr. Arora, receiving the good wishes of all the relatives. All Indian brides have to look sweet and innocent. It's their job. Auntie was very good at it, I thought admiringly. She did sweet and innocent in a very convincing way.

Dad was circulating, being congratulated on marrying his sister off to a catch like Mr. Arora. This was almost too much for Dad, the softie, to bear. His eyes were looking suspiciously moist.

"Girls!" shouted Auntie-ji, who had materialized out of thin air like a plump and cheery genie. "I haven't seen you for ages!" She grabbed us and hugged us one by one.

"How are things at the community center?" asked Geena.

Auntie-ji's face lit up. "Oh, there's so much to do!" she exclaimed joyously. "I've taken over the organization of the mum and baby group, and I help with meals for pensioners, and I drive the minibus, and—oh, all sorts of things!"

She looked completely fulfilled, and her round face

radiated contentment and goodwill. I felt extraordinarily pleased with myself.

There was a kerfuffle at the door, which was Uncle Dave, Auntie Rita and our cousins, Jaggi, Sukhvinder, Bobby and Baby, arriving with Biji, their gran.

"Where's Susie?" Auntie Rita bellowed at top volume. "I can't wait to meet this supposedly gorgeous young man she's marrying! Oh!" She caught sight of Mr. Arora sitting next to Auntie, and her mouth fell open. "Is *that* him?" She dropped her voice slightly but we could still hear her on the other side of the room. "How on earth did Susie manage to get her claws into *him*?"

"No good ever came of marrying a handsome man," Biji muttered darkly. "Ugly men are much more reliable." She banged her stick on the floor, just missing Dad's big toe. "Doesn't anyone here have a cup of tea for a thirsty old lady?"

Baby, who had always been one of our bitterest enemies, was causing quite a stir. She was poured into a long, silky pink skirt that sat low on her hips, and a matching top that knotted under her bosom, pushing it up and out quite a long way.

Jazz eyed her with dislike, and Auntie-ji was also looking very disapproving.

"Hello," I said as Baby walked across the room, showing off her wiggle. "That's a nice top you're almost wearing."

"Miaow," Baby purred. "Can I help the way I look?"

"Yes," said Auntie-ji, very unexpectedly. "You could stop putting all the goods in the shop window for a start. Men may like to rummage in the bargain basement, but in the end they always prefer to go for something a bit more upmarket."

Then she marched off, leaving Baby looking disgusted and me, Geena and Jazz giggling helplessly.

"Who's that rude old bag?" Baby snarled.

"Mr. Arora's auntie," I replied, "and don't talk about her like that."

"Oh, yeah, Mr. Arora," Baby went on. "Tell me, how did Auntie manage to land a gorgeous babe like *him*?"

"Auntie may be lucky to get Mr. Arora," I said sharply, "but he's just as lucky to be getting *her*."

Baby tittered. "Oh, come off it. She's hardly Miss World. I mean, she could do with losing a few pounds for a start—"

The three of us stepped forward as one.

"Why don't you leave our auntie alone and shove off before we dunk your head in the chicken curry?" Geena suggested.

Baby sniffed. "I don't know why you're so fond of her all of a sudden," she snapped. "I remember a time not so long ago when you didn't like her much yourself."

And off she tottered on her five-inch stiletto heels.

"Do you think that's true?" asked Jazz. "*Are* we fond of Auntie now?"

"I think so," I replied. We'd been so preoccupied with Rocky, the bet and Kiran that we'd almost forgotten that Auntie would be moving out soon. Next

146

week, in fact. "It's going to be strange not having her at home, isn't it?"

Geena and Jazz looked glum. A space had cleared at the table, but chicken curry and rice had suddenly lost its appeal.

"Dad hasn't said anything more about getting a housekeeper," Geena said hopefully. "Maybe he's going to see how we get along."

"I expect Auntie will pop round quite a bit," I pointed out. "They'll only be a twenty-minute drive away if they're living here. And you can't expect her to give up interfering in our lives completely. It would be unnatural."

"But when she and Mr. Arora buy their own house, they could be miles away," Jazz replied.

"Oh, why don't we just admit it," I said. "We're going to miss her. It'll be nice not to have her interfering and being one step ahead of our every move. But we're still going to miss her."

Geena and Jazz nodded. And so it happened that Dad was no longer the only person in the room with suspiciously damp eyes.

chapter 10

"You're looking good," I told Kiran very innocently. It was Monday morning, the bell had just rung for morning break time and we were packing away our books after history with Mr. Lucas. "Has anything happened?"

I know. I wasn't going to say anything to Kiran. But my curiosity about her and Rocky was getting the better of me. Beside me Kim cleared her throat very noisily. I ignored her.

"Happened?" Kiran slid her books into her bag. I wondered if she was avoiding looking at me on purpose. "What do you mean?"

"Well, I just noticed that you seem a lot happier," I replied.

Kim elbowed me in the ribs. I elbowed her back, harder.

"Things are easier at home," Kiran replied,

swinging her bag onto her shoulder. "We've had the house decorated, and we've unpacked and settled in." She grinned. "And the baby's sleeping through the night now, which helps."

"Sure." I followed her outside. Kim was poking me in the back, which was rather painful. "And?"

"And me and my mum have got more time to talk about Dad," Kiran went on. "You were right. It's better to talk than keep it all inside."

"I'm glad," I said, and meant it. "Is that all?"

Kiran frowned. "What do you mean?"

"Well . . . *ow!*" Kim had just poked me particularly viciously in the spine. "Oh, nothing."

"I'll see you outside in a minute, then." And Kiran disappeared into the girls' toilets.

"There was no need for that," I snapped, turning on Kim.

"I was trying to stop you from making a fool of yourself," Kim said in a saintly manner. "*And* from annoying Kiran. If she wants to talk about her feelings for Rocky, she will."

"I only wanted to help," I muttered sulkily.

"No, you were just sticking your nose in because you want to know what's going on," Kim said with deadly accuracy (I wasn't about to admit it, though).

I sighed as we went out into the playground. "I can't believe you think *that* of me after knowing me for eight years, Kim," I said.

"It's *because* I've known you for eight years that I can tell exactly what you're up to," Kim replied.

I really felt that this might have developed into a full-blown argument if we hadn't walked straight into a bust-up between, of all people, Rocky Gill and George Botley.

What happened was this. George was playing football with a gang of boys from our year. As Kim and I walked out of school, George was running backward to head a high ball. He crashed straight into Rocky, who wasn't looking where he was going either, and didn't hear anything because he had his headphones on.

"You idiot!" yelled Rocky. Those were not his *exact* words, you understand. They were a good deal ruder. "Get out of my way!"

He gave George a hefty shove. George staggered and went flying, landing in a large, deep puddle. Dirty water splashed everywhere, soaking his sweatshirt and trousers.

"Right!" George scrambled to his feet, his face bright red, fists clenched. "I've had enough of you!"

"Fight, fight, fight!"

Testosterone levels soared as all the males who were watching began baying for blood.

"I think not," I said briskly, stepping between the two of them. "George, come into school with me, and I'll help you clean up."

George looked reluctant, but I grabbed his soaking wet arm and dragged him away. The crowd of boys looked disappointed.

"Amber's just saved you from getting a pasting,

Botley," Rocky yelled as George and I went into school. "Stay away from me, you moron."

George turned a darker red. He tried to pull away from me, but I hung on with both hands. Kim, who was bringing up the rear, hurriedly closed the outside door behind us.

"That guy's a complete and total prat," George ranted as Kim and I escorted him down the corridor to our classroom. There was a washbasin in the corner, and while I filled it with warm water, Kim handed George some paper towels. "I just don't know what you see in him, Amber."

"Who said I see anything in him?" I muttered.

But George was so worked up, he wasn't listening. "Someone said he's going to play at your auntie's wedding," he went on. "You must be crazy!"

That did annoy me. "Why?" I said sharply. "Rocky's into bhangra and hip-hop, he writes his own stuff and he DJs too. He's got his own studio at home. He wants to do it professionally when he's older."

"Have you heard him?" George snapped.

"Well—no," I admitted. "Have you?"

"No." George stared crossly at me. "But just because he's handsome, it doesn't mean he's any *good*."

"That's true," Kim agreed.

"Oh, be quiet," I said.

George's remarks had worried me slightly. Oh, it wasn't that I didn't have faith in Rocky's ability. But maybe it *would* be better to get some idea of what he was actually planning to do at the wedding. Some hip-hop lyrics could be a bit—well—near the bone. I didn't want elderly aunties fainting away and ruining the reception. I was 99 percent sure I could trust Rocky. But still . . . It would be better to find out exactly what he was going to do.

And it was remarkably easy to arrange. After Kim and I had cleaned George up, we went outside to find Rocky with Geena, Jazz and Kiran. I sent George safely away in the opposite direction and went over to them. Geena and Jazz were, of course, ready with some tiresome and suggestive remarks about me and George, which I treated with the contempt they deserved. Then I launched straight in and asked Rocky if we could hear the stuff he planned to do at the wedding.

"Sure, no problem," Rocky agreed. "Why don't you all come round to my place tonight after school? I'll play you a set."

"We'll have to tell Auntie," Geena said, taking out her phone. "I'll give her a ring."

Kiran was shaking her head. "Sorry, I can't," she said, quite abruptly. "I've got something else on."

I glanced sideways at her. She had rather a strange look on her face. Was she jealous? I couldn't quite tell. . . .

I'd already guessed that Rocky's family was very well-off, but even I hadn't guessed just how posh they were. Their house in Temple Avenue had a drive the size of our back garden at home. The silver Mercedes and a white van were parked in front of the enormous house, and there was a black BMW in the open garage.

"We'll go straight to my studio," Rocky said casually. He led us to a flight of stairs next to the garage, and up to an apartment that was bigger than our living room. It was filled with recording equipment, lights, record decks, speakers and shelves and racks full of CDs and records. There were also a couple of plush, velvety designer sofas, as well as a tiny kitchen.

"There must be hundreds of pounds' worth of equipment here," Kim whispered in my ear. Her eyes were out on stalks.

"Make yourselves at home." Rocky opened the silver fridge and handed round cans of Coke. "I've just got to set things up."

We sank down onto the comfy sofa cushions, clutching our drinks, as Rocky put on a pair of headphones. I, for one, felt as if we'd wandered into a copy of *Hello!* magazine and were living a celebrity lifestyle.

"This is fabulous," Geena sighed. "It's the kind of thing I was born for."

"Money doesn't make you happy," Kim said piously.

"No," I agreed, "but at least you can be miserable in luxury."

"I wonder what the rest of the house is like," Jazz said, her eyes gleaming greedily.

"All right, you chicks." Rocky pointed a finger at us. "We're ready to rock!"

Geena's face darkened. *"Chicks?"* she repeated in a scathing tone.

"Shhh!" I hissed.

"All right, bhangra-loving dudes, listen up. This is the one and only Rocket Man!"

A loud, thumping bass began to pour out of the massive speakers behind us, almost blowing our heads off with a remixed bhangra version of "Eye of the Tiger." Rocky began dancing around behind his desks while we watched, mesmerized.

"And I'm here today to play you some thumping tracks that are gonna blow this roof off! These tracks are bee-yoo-ti-ful—almost as beautiful as the bride!"

"He's a bit cheesy, isn't he?" said Kim doubtfully as Rocky went through some dance moves behind the decks.

"It's a wedding, Kim," I replied. "A bit of cheese is OK."

Rocky treated us to a bit more of his DJ patter, then stopped the music abruptly. He grinned at us. "I'll do one of the raps I wrote last week," he said eagerly. "It's called 'No Time for School.'"

We all clapped politely as a backing track with a bhangra beat began to blare out. Rocky raised the mike and went for it.

> *"I ain't got no time for school,*
> *I ain't got no time for history,*
> *I ain't got no time for geography,*
> *I ain't got no time for A to Z . . ."*

Now, I know a bit about bhangra. I know something about rap and hip-hop. However, you didn't need to know anything about music at all to realize straight away that Rocky was—how shall I put this?—utter *rubbish*.

Was it possible to rap out of tune? I wouldn't have said so before this. But, apparently, it was.

The lyrics were not lyrical in any sense of the word. Rocky was no Eminem. All the tired old rhymes were there: *school/rule/cool/fool*.

During one particularly poor interlude (when Rocky boasted about how his rapping would make even the teachers dance—something I very much doubted), I glanced at Geena, Jazz and Kim. Their appalled faces mirrored exactly what I was feeling. It might have been funny, if Rocky wasn't planning to perform in public.

And I knew then that there was absolutely no way I could let him play at Auntie's wedding.

chapter 11

"Well?" Rocky laid down the mike and looked at us eagerly. "What do you think?"

I felt sorry for him. It wasn't only that I didn't want Auntie's wedding reception to be ruined. I was also thinking of Rocky. He'd be laughed off the stage. And possibly pelted with bits of the wedding feast, too.

"Amber, do something," Geena whispered pleadingly in my ear. "Say something. Anything."

"Rocky, that was great," I said. I felt Kim fidgeting beside me and hoped she wasn't about to go into her lying-shows-a-lack-of-integrity speech. "But there's something you need to know. I just wasn't sure how to tell you. . . ."

Rocky frowned. "What?"

"This had better be good, Amber," Jazz muttered out of the side of her mouth.

I took a breath. "Well, when Geena phoned Auntie to let her know we'd be home late, Auntie told her that there'd been a mix-up with the arrangements for the reception."

"She did?" said Geena. "I mean, yes, she did."

"What kind of mix-up?" asked Rocky, his eyes narrowing.

"Er—Mr. Arora's auntie has booked the Bhangra Boyz to perform at the reception," I said, silently giving thanks to Auntie-ji. I'd never complain when she hugged me again, not even if she broke every bone in my body.

Rocky burst out laughing. "What, that bunch of old has-beens? I'll blow them off the stage!" He swaggered out from behind the decks, still laughing. "If they want to play a few songs, I don't care. It'll be a laugh!"

"Er—you don't understand," I said. "Auntie-ji has booked them for the whole evening. There won't be any time for you to play or DJ." I crossed my fingers, hoping I would be forgiven for my second lie in three minutes. And also hoping that the Boyz *would* be willing to play a longer set if Auntie-ji asked them to.

Rocky's face darkened. "What!" he roared. "But we had a deal!"

"I know," I said. "I'm sorry."

Jazz squeezed my arm. Geena was looking relieved.

"See?" I whispered to Kim. "Sometimes lying is the only way."

"I'm not going to argue," Kim whispered back. "Well done."

Rocky had turned an interesting shade of purple. "No," he said angrily.

"What do you mean—no?" I asked.

"We had a deal, and I'm sticking to it." Rocky glared at me. "You'd better do the same."

"But I just told you—" I began.

Rocky shrugged. "Not my problem," he said flatly. "I'm playing at your aunt's wedding, and that's that. You sort it out."

I gritted my teeth. "I can't," I snapped. "I already told you."

"All right." Rocky's eyes narrowed. "If you won't keep your part of the deal, then I don't have to keep mine."

A cold feeling of dread washed over me. "What do you mean?"

"I mean I'll tell Kiran that I only made friends with her because *you* asked me to," Rocky said spitefully. "I'll tell her that you three were fed up with her. I'll tell her that nobody liked her until I started hanging out with her. And that if I stop being mates with her, she won't have any friends at all."

We stared at him in horror.

"You unfeeling monster," Kim muttered.

"You wouldn't do that," I said.

"And I reckon she fancies me as well," Rocky went on with a smug grin. I could happily have slapped his handsome face at this moment. "So if you don't want her to be *really* upset, you know what to do."

"And to think we believed you actually *liked* Kiran," Geena said in a contemptuous voice.

Rocky suddenly looked a little less smug and a lot more awkward. "I do," he admitted.

"How much?" I asked hopefully. If Rocky really did like Kiran, appealing to his better nature could be the only way. Although I was beginning to suspect that he didn't actually have one. "A lot?"

"Yeah, I like her." Rocky shrugged. "But if you mean would I go out with her—no. She's not my type."

"I should think not," said Kim. "She's bright and funny and intelligent and smart."

Rocky ignored her. "If Kiran was six inches shorter and a lot slimmer and a bit prettier, then yeah, I might consider it," he said thoughtfully. "She's OK as a mate. But not as a girlfriend. She's just not good for my image."

"She's had a lucky escape, then," Kim muttered.

"You wouldn't really tell Kiran about our deal?" I asked desperately.

"No, I won't," Rocky replied, "*if* I get to play at your aunt's wedding."

There didn't seem to be anything more to say. Gloomily we trailed out of the studio. Rocky didn't seem at all fazed, and even gave us a cheery wave as we left.

"How can someone so beautiful be so awful?" Jazz wailed.

"Shakespeare summed it up very well," said Geena pompously. "Some quote about the canker in the bud. Unfortunately I can't quite remember it at the moment."

"Never mind Shakespeare," I said. "*What* are we going to do?"

"Could we maybe tell Rocky just how truly vile his singing is?" suggested Kim. "That might make him stop."

Geena shook her head. "He'd never believe us."

"He's a bighead," I murmured, thinking of George Botley with some fondness. If it hadn't been for him, I wouldn't have found out how terrible Rocky's performance was until he actually turned up at Auntie's wedding. The thought brought me out in a cold sweat.

"Well, it's Monday today, and the wedding's on Sunday," Geena said anxiously. "We've got five days to try to persuade him to do the decent thing."

"What do you think our chances of success are?" asked Jazz.

"Nil," Geena replied glumly. "Maybe we should just let him play at the wedding anyway. He'd be laughed off the stage, and it'd serve him right."

"But then Auntie's special day would be ruined," Jazz pointed out. "We can't let that happen."

"Maybe we can stop Rocky playing anyway," I said slowly.

"How?" asked Kim.

"By making sure he doesn't turn up at the wedding reception."

"And we do that how?" Jazz wanted to know.

"Well, at the moment my only idea is to kidnap him and lock him in a dark cellar somewhere," I replied. "But I'm working on it."

chapter 12

However, I'm sorry to say that four days later, ideas were still very, very thin on the ground.

"We could sabotage the electrics," Jazz suggested. "If there's no power, then Rocky won't be able to play."

"So we spend the whole of the wedding reception sitting in the dark?" scoffed Geena. "That's just about your worst idea yet, Jazz."

"No, I thought the worst was telling Rocky he had been selected for the next series of *Pop Idol*, and he had to go to the TV studios right away," I said.

"Really?" Kim looked surprised. "I thought the one about moving the wedding reception to a top-secret location at the last minute was pretty awful."

Jazz looked annoyed. "Well, at least I'm *trying*," she

snapped. "It might have escaped your notice, but it's Friday afternoon and the wedding's on Sunday and we still haven't figured out a way to stop Rocky."

Jazz was perfectly right, of course. The last four days had been spent trying to appeal to Rocky's better nature. I now knew for sure that he definitely did not have one. Not that Rocky bore a grudge against us. He was as friendly as ever, to both us and Kiran. But he had only one thing set in his sights that mattered to him. Rocky Gill was going to be a star, and the first stepping-stone to success was Auntie's wedding reception.

"This is our last chance to see him before Sunday," said Geena as we waited around at the playground gates, watching everyone else head for home. "Unless we go round to his house tomorrow and beg him on bended knee to pull out."

"It might very well come to that," I replied.

At that moment Rocky came out of school. Unfortunately, he was with Kiran.

I said a mildly rude word under my breath.

"Well, that's it, then," Jazz said gloomily. "We're done for. Hung, drawn and quartered. Or we will be by Sunday evening."

"Everything all right?" asked George Botley, who was hanging around nearby.

"Nothing for you to worry your pretty little head about, George." I managed a smile. "See you."

George raised a hand. "Hope the wedding goes off OK," he called as he walked away.

I winced. "So do we," I muttered as Rocky and Kiran

strolled toward us. "But at the moment there's about a one percent chance of that happening."

"Hey, girls!" Rocky grinned jauntily at us. "Looking forward to Sunday? I know I am!"

We all glared at him. However, it was like water off a very stupid duck's back.

"Kiran's coming over tomorrow to hear me run through my set," Rocky went on. "She hasn't heard me play before."

"Oh, my, Kiran," said Geena. "Have you got a treat in store."

Kiran grinned at us. "Yeah? And I've got a surprise for *you* as well."

I was immediately intrigued. "What?"

"You'll find out soon," Kiran replied. "Maybe sooner than you think!"

We watched the two of them walk off together.

"What surprise is that then?" asked Jazz.

"It'll be something to do with Rocky," replied Geena. "Maybe she thinks he's going to ask her out. Or maybe she's going to ask *him* out."

"Don't say that," I muttered with a feeling of dread. "Oh, why has everything gone so wrong?"

Kim opened her mouth to reply. But she didn't get a chance because I clapped my hand over it.

"Thank you, Kim," I said. "I already know that this is mostly my fault."

"Mostly?" Geena and Jazz said together.

"All right," I admitted. "*All* my fault."

"Never mind," Jazz said kindly. "I'm sure you'll be

punished enough when Auntie hears Rocky play at her wedding reception."

"That's a certainty," I replied gloomily.

Friday evening through to Saturday evening was a whirlwind of activity. Even if I'd wanted to go and fling myself at Rocky's feet and beg him tearfully to reconsider, I didn't have time.

Almost every female relative in the family arrived at our house on Saturday. Some of them immediately took over the kitchen and started cooking huge vats of curry and millions of samosas, pakoras and bhajis. We did have wedding caterers, but the idea of running out of food for the ravenous hordes (sorry, wedding guests) was too much to bear, so we stockpiled enough to feed the whole of southeast England in an emergency. Others (like Auntie Rita) sat around gossiping, and others (like Biji) sat around criticizing. One sat around painting her nails (that was Baby). It was traditional pre-wedding chaos. Dad ran off to the office in a panic, and we didn't see him for hours.

Later on, after we'd eaten, there was singing and dancing in the living room. We pushed back the furniture, and most of the women danced around, singing mildly rude songs about the groom, the bride and the wedding night.

"It'll be your turn soon, Geena," cackled several aunties as they lumbered around the living room floor.

Geena forced a smile, then pulled a face at me and

Jazz. "And I think I can safely say that Rocky won't be playing at *my* wedding reception," she whispered.

"Why did you have to remind me?" I groaned. "I was enjoying myself so much."

What made me feel worse than ever was that Auntie was having such a great time. She was glowing with happiness, although remembering to look suitably sad and sweet when any old aunties and grannies were around. Indian brides are supposed to look upset at leaving the family home when they get married. Auntie was doing her best to toe the line, but a smile *would* keep breaking out every so often. I didn't think she'd have any trouble keeping a straight face at the wedding reception, though—once Rocky started playing, she'd be doing her best not to burst into tears.

There was more fun and games as Auntie's hands and feet were decorated with mehndi, and she was given the traditional twenty-one red and cream wedding bangles to wear. Afterward, some of the relatives started to drift off home. The other fifteen or so were staying the night with us. Jazz and I had been unceremoniously ejected from our bedroom and were bunking in with Geena. A fiercely contested pillow fight had ensured that I got to share Geena's double bed, while Jazz was stuck with the creaky camp bed on the floor.

"If you and Geena weren't so mean," Jazz grumbled, climbing into her pajamas, "I could get in at the other end."

"Which means we'd have to sleep with your feet in our faces," replied Geena. "Forget it."

"I'll be worrying about Rocky all night," I muttered, snuggling under the duvet. "I bet I don't get any sleep."

"Well, you might as well have the camp bed, then," Jazz said hopefully.

There was a tap at the door.

"Not asleep yet, girls?" Auntie poked her head round the door. She was wrapped in her dressing gown.

"You should be getting your beauty sleep for tomorrow," Geena said severely.

Auntie came in and closed the door. "I've got to wait a bit longer for this to harden before I wash it off," she said, waving her hands at us. The henna paste was the color of dried mud. "So I thought I'd come and say good night. As this is the last time I'll be here."

"We should be so lucky," I joked.

"All right." Auntie smiled. "I mean, the last time I'll be living here."

There was a short silence.

"It hasn't been so bad, has it?" asked Geena.

"It got better," Auntie replied. "The first few months were horrible."

"Yes, for us too," I said. I wasn't joking this time.

"But once I found some rather lovely girls underneath the spoilt little brats, I think we got along fine," Auntie went on. "Your mum had written and told me how wonderful you all were, so I knew I had to keep trying."

I was horrified to find tears pricking my eyes. "Well, as soon as we found out you could cook, we decided to keep you on," I said. My voice wobbled a bit at the end.

"I'm just sorry I'm leaving when we've started to get on so well," Auntie said shakily.

"But Mr. Arora's so l-l-lovely," Jazz stammered, a single tear rolling down her cheek. "You couldn't turn him down."

"No." Auntie gulped. "Not after the three of you went to so much trouble to get us together."

"I hate goodbyes," Geena mumbled.

"I'm going to miss you all," Auntie sobbed.

We gathered on the bed and had a group hug.

"I'm not going to be far away," Auntie reassured us. "We'll still see each other most days."

"It won't be the same, though," I wept. "You won't be here when we get home from school."

"And when you and Mr. Arora buy your own house," sobbed Geena, "you might move miles away."

"We won't," Auntie promised.

Jazz sniffed. "Can I ask you something?"

"Anything."

"How did you always know when we were listening outside the living room door?"

"If the door was open a little way, I could see your reflections in the mirror in the hall," Auntie replied, wiping her eyes.

We stopped sobbing and started laughing.

"Well, that explains *that*," I said.

"It's time we all got some sleep." Auntie gave us all one last quick hug. "We've got a big day ahead of us tomorrow."

I felt my heart sinking, sinking, sinking right down to my feet. I did not see how I could possibly enjoy the wedding, knowing the horrors in store at the reception. Geena and Jazz looked suitably depressed too.

I didn't sleep very well that night. It felt like I didn't sleep *at all*. Every time Jazz turned over, the camp bed creaked. I'd whisper, "Shut up!" and then Geena would elbow me in the ribs. This seemed to happen every five minutes.

The whole house was awake and buzzing by five-thirty. We tried stuffing our fingers in our ears and sticking our heads under our pillows, but nothing could muffle the sound of high-pitched excited chattering. So in the end we got up too.

We looked fabulous in our new outfits, even if Jazz's pale pink skirt *was* slit a little too high. But although I felt ultraglamorous in my aquamarine suit with matching silky scarf and high-heeled silver sandals, I just could not relax and enjoy myself.

All the relatives started crying and showering blessings on Auntie as she was escorted downstairs by Dad. Although she kept her eyes down, like a proper Indian bride, she looked stunning. Her red silk sari, heavily embroidered with gold, had cost a whole shed load of money, but it was worth it, and she was dripping with gold jewelry from her head right down to her feet.

"You look great too, Dad," I said as we waited outside for the wedding car to arrive.

Dad winced. "This is the first and last time I buy an Armani suit," he replied. "I had to sit down when I wrote the check."

"Hey, what about when *we* get married?" said Jazz. "You'll want to look good then, won't you?"

"Don't worry," Dad replied, "I shall be wearing this suit for the next twenty years, after what it cost me."

"You'd better not put on any weight, then," remarked Geena.

Dad grinned. "Remind me not to eat too much at the reception. The food looks fantastic."

I sagged despondently as a white limo, decorated with flowers, purred down the street toward us. The reception . . . for a minute there I'd forgotten all about it.

We set off for the gurdwara. When I was a little kid, I remembered how long the marriage service had seemed. I'd get bored very quickly, and Mum would sometimes let Geena and me go outside and play until it was over. But now it all seemed very quick. Too quick. Mr. Arora was waiting for Auntie, looking like a movie star in his pink turban, white suit and saffron-colored scarf. People came in, bowed to the Holy Book and took their places on each side of the aisle. Then the granthi, the holy man, began the ceremony.

As the marriage hymn was sung, Auntie and Mr. Arora walked around the Guru Granth Sahib, the

Holy Book, each holding one end of the orange scarf. Then there were prayers, and it was all over.

"We could hit Rocky over the head and knock him out," Jazz suggested as we came out of the gurdwara into the autumn sunshine.

"And if we accidentally killed him?" Geena raised her eyebrows. "That would certainly ruin Auntie's day."

I sighed. "There's nothing more we can do," I said. "We'll just have to hope everyone thinks he's a comedy act. Then we might just get away with it."

I felt sick with nerves as we made our way to the reception. Rocky would be waiting there for us. Either he had improved tremendously in the last five days, or he was going to bring the house down, and not in a good way. I just hoped Auntie would be able to forgive me.

chapter 13

The reception was held in a large community hall, not far from the gurdwara. Garlands of sweet-scented flowers had been hung around the doors, and the hall had been decorated with more flowers—red and white carnations and roses—and streamers. The waiters were already rushing out from the kitchens and placing silver dishes of nuts and sweets on the tables, which were set out around the stage.

The stage. My heart jumped painfully in my chest as I peered across the hall. The Bhangra Boyz's instruments were set up, ready for them to perform, but they had left a large space at the side of the stage for Rocky's decks.

The space was still there. And that was what it was. An empty space.

171

"Geena," I said faintly, clutching her arm.

"Ow!" Geena grumbled. "You're hurting me."

"Tell me if I'm seeing things," I muttered. "But Rocky's equipment isn't there, is it?"

Geena stared. "Oh, my God," she said in amazement. "He hasn't turned up!"

My heart soared upward again. "I don't believe it!"

Jazz joined us then, her eyes wide. "I thought Rocky was supposed to be coming a couple of hours ago to set up," she said.

"He hasn't turned up!" Geena and I sang together. We grabbed Jazz's hands and danced her round the hall.

Guests were crowding in through the doors now. I saw Kim come in, looking very pretty in the blue salwar kameez I'd lent her.

"Auntie and Mr. Arora are just getting out of the limo," she called, making her way over to us. "Auntie looks lovely."

"I know." I beamed at her. "Notice anything?"

Kim looked blank. I pointed at the stage.

"Oh!" Kim's eyes opened wide. "Where's Rocky?"

"He's not here!" I chortled, slapping her on the back. "We're saved!"

"Well, where is he, then?" Kim wanted to know.

"Oh, who cares?" said Geena. "The further away the better."

"That wasn't what you said a few weeks ago," Kim remarked.

We blushed.

"All right," I said. "So you were right about Rocky and we were wrong. He turned out to be a bit of a disappointment."

"It's not like he's evil or anything," Geena agreed. "Just a bit dull and self-centered."

"What a waste," Jazz sighed. "I wonder which one of us he *did* like best, though."

"I hereby declare that ridiculous bet null and void as of this very minute," I announced.

"We could still ask him," Jazz began.

"No!" Geena and I told her firmly.

Auntie-ji hurried past us, rearranging flowers with one hand, straightening a tablecloth with the other and scolding a waiter at the same time. She screeched to a halt when she spotted us.

"Amber, where's your friend?" she asked with a frown. "He's very late."

"He's not coming," I said, trying to smother an enormous grin. "Sorry."

Auntie-ji looked shocked. "You mean, he's let us down at the last minute?" she exclaimed. "That's terrible!"

"I know," I agreed, still trying not to smile. "But we could ask the Bhangra Boyz if they'd like to play a longer set."

Auntie-ji nodded. "That's a very good idea, Amber," she said, sounding relieved. "And I'm sure some of our guests will be able to rustle up a few CDs so we can have some background music."

And she bustled off, delighted to have yet another crisis to deal with.

Now, at last, I could relax and enjoy the wedding. There were cheers and applause as Auntie and Mr. Arora came in, and then it was down to the serious business of eating. Huge pots of chicken, vegetable and paneer curries were placed on the tables along with towers of chapatis and enormous bowls of rice. And a quick whip-round of all the guests produced a pile of CDs from their cars and a portable CD player.

"There's Mrs. Macey." I pointed my fork at the door. Our neighbor had arrived from Southampton with her family—her daughter and son-in-law and two sweet little grandchildren.

Kim nudged me. "I've been meaning to ask you," she whispered. "Who's *that*?"

We followed her gaze to a table across the room, where Baby was sitting with her family.

"Oh, you've never had the pleasure of meeting our cousin Baby, have you?" I said.

"*Baby?*" Kim looked disapproving. "She must be at least nineteen."

"Fifteen, actually," Geena replied. "And if she's not careful she's going to burst out of that white suit she's wearing."

Baby's wedding outfit consisted of a skin-tight pair of white trousers, skyscraper gold heels and a white halter top decorated with gold sequins. The clothes looked as if they were sprayed on and would have to be surgically removed.

I pointed beyond Baby's table as someone else

caught my eye. "Who's that woman over there with all the kids?" I asked. "Do we know her?"

"Hello," said a familiar voice in my ear.

It was Kiran—looking pretty and feminine for once, in a light green suit, with a white flower in her hair.

We stared at her in disbelief.

"Wh-What are *you* doing here?" I stammered.

Kiran raised an eyebrow at us. "That's nice," she said with a grin. "I *was* invited."

"By whom?" asked Geena, looking nervous.

The same thought had occurred to me. Maybe Rocky had asked her along to help with his equipment! I gulped, scanning the room with dread. But there was still no sign of him.

"Mr. Arora's auntie asked us," Kiran explained. "My mum and the others are over there."

She pointed at the woman I'd just noticed. Now I could see that it was Kiran's mum. But she looked so different—dressed up and made up—that I hadn't recognized her.

"This is getting more and more confusing," Jazz grumbled. "How do you know Auntie-ji?"

"Oh, she's been *great*," replied Kiran. "We met her at the community center in Shepherd Road. She's really sorted us out. She organized people to do our decorating, and she's helped Mum with the kids. And she babysits so that Mum can get out and make friends. She's made a big difference."

"Why didn't you mention this before?" I asked.

Kiran shrugged. "I didn't find out she was Mr. Arora's auntie until yesterday," she explained. "I had a feeling I'd seen her before, but I couldn't remember where. Anyway, she's been amazing."

"So *that's* why you've been looking happier over the last few weeks," I said, feeling mightily relieved that maybe, just maybe, Kiran wasn't in love with Rocky after all.

Kiran nodded. "Auntie-ji told me yesterday that it was your idea for her to volunteer at the community center," she said. "I owe you one, Amber. I can't tell you how much she's done for us."

"We thought you were happier because you were in love with Rocky," Jazz blurted out in her usual thoughtful manner.

Kiran's eyes opened wide. Then she began to roar with laughter.

"Obviously not," I said, feeling even more relieved.

"Are you *kidding*?" Kiran chuckled. "I mean, he's nice enough and I get on well with him, especially when we're talking about music. But he can be a bit immature. And boy, doesn't he think he's great! He's OK as a mate, but that's as far as it goes."

"Have you heard him do his bhangra rap?" asked Jazz.

Kiran shuddered. "I went round to his house yesterday," she said. "It nearly killed me. I did actually try to persuade him not to come today."

"So you're the reason he didn't turn up!" I threw Kiran a grateful look. "Thanks ever so much."

But Kiran was shaking her head. "He wouldn't listen to me," she said. "He was determined to come, one way or another."

"So why isn't he here?" asked Kim.

"Oh, never mind." I pushed a chair toward Kiran. "Sit down with us and have something to eat."

Rocky's no-show was a mystery, but it wasn't something I was going to worry my head over. No doubt I'd find out the reason behind it at school on Monday.

But actually, I didn't have to wait that long. I'd left the hall, where the Bhangra Boyz had just started playing, and was on my way down the corridor to the ladies'. The outside doors were open, and as I passed them, a panting and disheveled figure rushed in.

"Rocky!" I gasped in horror. "What the hell are you doing here? I mean, where have you been?"

Rocky slapped his forehead, looking totally flustered. "You're not going to believe this!" he groaned. "Dad and I loaded all my gear into the van. Somehow it got locked and we couldn't find the keys, and then Dad didn't know where the spares were." He stared at me, wild-eyed. "So the van is still sitting on our drive and I haven't got any equipment, but maybe the band will let me do a few songs? They could play for me."

"Well, I don't know about that," I said quickly. "I'll have to go and check. Wait here."

"Thanks, Amber." Looking a little more cheerful, Rocky slid his arm round my shoulder and gave me a squeeze. "Listen, I know about that bet you, Geena and Jazz made. . . ."

"Oh, really?" I muttered, embarrassed.

"And I want you to know that, of the three of you, I like *you* best," Rocky whispered in my ear.

And now I'd gone and declared the bet null and void. Drat. But apart from losing a couple of slaves for a day, I wasn't at all thrilled, to be honest.

"You know, maybe we could get together for a slow dance at the end of my set," Rocky went on, looking more and more pleased with himself.

"You'll have to get past my dad first," I replied, easing myself free. "Wait here."

I went back into the hall, my brain operating on red alert. I headed straight for Baby.

"Baby," I said quietly, "I need your help."

Baby yawned and put down the chapati she was nibbling. "What's in it for me?"

"My silver DKNY sunglasses," I replied. "The ones you've had your eye on for the last six months."

Baby's mask of sophistication fell away instantly. "Are you serious?" she gasped.

I nodded. "There's a boy outside," I went on. "I want him kept away from the stage by whatever means are necessary. I'll leave that up to you."

Baby glared at me. "He's fat and spotty with sweaty hands, I suppose?" she sneered.

"See for yourself," I invited.

We went over to the door, and Baby peered out into the corridor.

"The guy in the leather jacket?" she asked in tones of utter disbelief. "What's the catch?"

"No catch," I said. "Just keep him away from the stage for the rest of the reception. That's all I ask."

"But—he's gorgeous!" Baby spluttered.

I shrugged. "Well, if you don't think you're up to it . . . ," I began, turning away.

Baby grabbed my arm. "Are you joking?" she whispered crossly. "Introduce me—now!"

We went over to Rocky. He might have liked me best about two minutes ago, but he didn't spare me a single glance now. His eyes were fixed on Baby's undulating curves.

"The band isn't sure if there'll be time for you to play," I said.

"But—" Rocky began.

"Don't worry." Baby took his arm, looking up at him from beneath her false eyelashes. "I'll look after you."

"This is my cousin, Baby," I said.

Rocky and Baby stared into each other's eyes. They were both spoilt and immature and had a high opinion of themselves. I guess they'd both found their soul mate.

"Come and have something to eat," Baby invited, and dragged him off into the hall.

I sighed hugely with relief. We were safe. I had no doubt at all that Baby would fulfill her side of the bargain.

I slipped outside into the cool air to take a few deep breaths. To my utter amazement, I came face to face with George Botley, who was loitering on the step. He stared at me in horror and tried to edge his way out of sight behind a large bush.

"George, what are you *doing* here?" I cried, grabbing his sleeve. He looked as if he'd been running. He was pink and panting.

"Nothing," George mumbled.

"Nothing," I repeated with pointed sarcasm. "You turn up at my aunt's wedding and lurk around outside and that's nothing? Let's have it."

George stared down at his trainers. "I was trying to stop Rocky from coming here."

"What?" I stared at him.

"I heard you talking about trying to stop him from singing at the reception." George took a bunch of keys out of his pocket and held them up. "So I—er—happened to be passing the Gills' house this morning while they were loading the van—"

"George!" I gasped. "You locked the van and took the keys?"

George nodded. "But Rocky came anyway. I followed him here, but I couldn't think how to stop him coming in."

I stared severely at him. "George, that was a very foolish thing to do," I scolded. "What if you'd been caught? I can't believe you've been so stupid."

George hung his head. While he wasn't looking at me, I allowed myself one big grin.

"Well, now that you're here, you'd better come in and have something to eat," I said briskly.

"But I'm not invited—" George began.

"You are now." This time I couldn't help smiling at him. "George, I'd be honored if you'd attend my aunt's wedding."

George brightened up quite considerably. We went inside together to find Geena, Jazz and Kim dancing around in a panic just outside the hall.

"Rocky's turned up," Jazz wailed. "What are we going to do?"

"At the moment Baby's distracting him," added Geena. "But we're not sure how long that will last."

"Hello, George," Kim said. "What are *you* doing here?"

"Relax," I said easily. "Everything's sorted."

Quickly I explained recent events. I'm sorry to say, however, that Jazz, Geena and Kim chose not to focus on my brilliance in preventing Rocky from taking to the stage. Instead they homed in on George's motives for taking the keys.

"You must like Amber a lot, George," Jazz said, smirking. "I mean, you might have been *arrested*."

"He must think Amber's worth it," Kim chimed in, enjoying my embarrassment.

"It's so romantic," Geena added.

"Oh, be quiet," I muttered as I led George over to our table. Kiran had returned to sit with her mum and Auntie-ji, and Rocky and Baby were absorbed in each other in a quiet corner.

"Well, of course I like Amber," George said coolly, sitting down. "And she knows I do." He flashed me a smile, and I have to admit my knees did wobble slightly.

"Is this your musical friend, Amber?" Dad appeared from nowhere, clutching a plate of paneer curry. He has this ability to materialize out of nowhere whenever there are boys around.

"No, he's otherwise engaged with Baby," I replied. "This is George, Dad. He's in my class at school."

George stood up and held out his hand, which impressed me no end.

"I hope your intentions are honorable, George," Dad said sternly. "I have a very strict vetting procedure for my daughters' would-be husbands."

George looked stunned.

"Dad!" I groaned.

Dad burst out laughing. "I'm kidding," he chuckled. "Well, not about the vetting procedure. But you're a bit young yet. Maybe in a few years' time."

"OK," George agreed.

"George!" I whispered crossly.

Dad wandered away, still laughing.

"Does this mean you and George are engaged?" Geena inquired, while Jazz and Kim giggled.

"No," I said.

"Yes," said George with a grin.

"You're getting a bit above yourself now, George," I retorted, handing him a plate.

I checked on Rocky and Baby, who were ignoring everyone around them. Rocky's leather jacket was draped over a chair nearby.

"Give me those keys, Georgie," I whispered. "I'm

going to slip them into Rocky's pocket while he's not looking."

I strolled innocently across the floor, dodging between the dancers, and dropped the keys into the jacket pocket as I walked past. Rocky and Baby were so busy staring into each other's eyes that they didn't notice me.

I made my way back across the dance floor to our table.

"Well, I don't know how you managed it, Amber," Geena remarked, "but everything seems to have turned out for the best, for once."

I shrugged. "I told you to have faith in my ideas."

George stopped eating chicken curry and cleared his throat rather pointedly.

"All right," I grumbled. "Thank you, George. You were a big help."

"This will be our first night without Auntie at home," Jazz said thoughtfully. "We'll be able to stay up late from now on, and do whatever we like."

"Takeaway pizza for dinner tomorrow?" suggested Geena.

I sighed happily. "It'll be just like old times."

"I can see you're going to miss Auntie heaps," Kim said sarcastically.

"Of course we will," I replied, "but we've got to make the best of it, haven't we?"

"Until Dad decides to get a housekeeper." Geena frowned. "We've got to make sure that doesn't happen. Maybe we can get Auntie on our side."

"Girls, are you having a good time?" Auntie and Mr. Arora were coming toward us, both looking flushed and happy. "Everything's going very well, isn't it?"

We nodded. Mr. Arora was staring at George with some surprise, but he didn't say anything.

"Auntie, has Dad said anything to you about looking for a housekeeper?" Geena asked. "Because, to be honest, we really think that we're old enough to look after ourselves now."

"Well, that's a matter of opinion," Auntie said with a smile. "But I can tell you that, no, your dad won't be hiring a housekeeper. He's decided not to."

We glanced at each other in delight but tried to make sure we didn't look too pleased. Auntie was quite capable of going off and changing Dad's mind for him.

"The thing is," Auntie went on, "we have some news for you." She and Mr. Arora (or should I call him Uncle Jai now?) smiled starrily at each other. "We've just been speaking to Mrs. Macey—Gloria—and she wants to move down to Southampton to be closer to her family. Her house is going up for sale."

"And guess who'll be buying it?" Mr. Arora added with a beaming smile.

We stared at them in disbelief.

"You two?" Geena squeaked.

Auntie nodded. "So I'll only be next door," she said with a grin. "Keeping an eye on you, just like I've been doing."

"Fantastic," I said weakly.

Just then the band struck up a particularly catchy bhangra tune, and Mr. Arora whirled Auntie onto the dance floor.

"Aren't you pleased?" asked Kim.

"Yes and no," I sighed.

"It will be great in some ways," Jazz agreed. "And not so great in others."

"Oh, well, so much for freedom," said Geena. "That's the trouble with interfering aunties. They never give up."

"True," agreed Jazz. "I feel sorry for our children, Geena."

"Why?" Geena wanted to know.

"Because their interfering auntie will be Amber," Jazz replied. "What a horrible thought."

"What you really mean is that your children will be the luckiest alive." I leaned over and reached for George's hand. "Come on, George. If you want to impress my dad, the first thing you've got to do is learn to dance bhangra style!"

About the Author

Narinder Dhami was born in Wolverhampton and now lives in Cambridge, England. After earning an English degree from Birmingham University, she began teaching in London in the early eighties. She worked as a primary school teacher for ten years, but for the past twelve years she has been a full-time writer. At first she wrote almost exclusively for children's magazines, and she has had almost two hundred short stories and articles published. But after a few years she concentrated on writing children's novels. Her previous books (many available only in the United Kingdom) include *Angel Face, Animal Crackers, Annie's Game, Changing Places* and the novelization of the hit movie *Bend It Like Beckham*. Check out her Web site at www.narinderdhami.com.